EARTH LOG

EARTH LOG

Blaine C. Readler

FULL ARC PRESS

EARTH LOG

This is a work of fiction. Names, characters, places and incidents are either the product of the author's wild imagination or are used fictitiously. Any resemblance to actual events, locales, organizations, or persons, living, dead, or one foot in the grave, although inevitable and in a weird way complimentary to the author, since it shows he is not so insulated from reality that the products of his imagination are totally alien to the average mind, is nevertheless entirely coincidental and beyond the intent of either the author or the publisher.

Visit us at: http://www.readler.com

E-mail: blaine@readler.com

ISBN: 978-0-9992296-3-7

Printed in the United States of America

To my brother, Ken, and my other brother, Joe.
Because they read all my books, probably even this one.

ACKNOWLEDGEMENTS

A heartfelt thanks to MTB for her continued dedication in containing my grammatical, typographical, and contextual fumbles.

A robust thanks to James Ward for once more manifesting a visual essence of a tale.
https://www.jameswardillustrations.com

The only way to have a friend is to be one.
—Ralph Waldo Emerson

Chapter 1

I am, apparently, a ferret. I know this because that's what Joanne calls me. Joanne is apparently my master. I know *this* because she scolds me when I root around in the cupboard, and then picks me up and puts me in a cage. She does this, confident that I won't resist. I can't, by the way. Resist, I mean. When she angrily grabs me, I feel an urge to nip her with my razor teeth, but am not able to act on the impulse, and this is apparently wired into my brain.

I know that's a lot of suppositions, but suppositions are all I have to go on. I have no memory beyond three days ago when I woke up. I opened my eyes and found myself lying in my little bed inside a cardboard box with a hole cut out of the side. It sits on the floor in the corner of Joanne's apartment. I had no memory of how I got there—no memory of anything, actually. Despite that, I somehow knew that this little bed is where I should be when I wake up, and that Joanne would be asleep in her bedroom, and that if I went in and jumped up on her bed, she would groan, and complain, but pull me in to cuddle, which I would let her do for about two minutes until my curiosity would draw me away.

All this built-in knowledge. It's like my conscious mind became decoupled, but the subconscious is still intact. A ferret's subconscious.

This is curious. Something tells me that a normal ferret shouldn't be thinking about conscious minds and the word "supposition." On the other hand, it feels normal to me. I am a ferret that mulls over aspects of partitioned memory.

Like all animals, ferrets are driven by instincts, and I am apparently no different. For example, I wouldn't think of sleeping anywhere except in my box, where I feel safe—a holdover from my ancient polecat ancestry, as Joanne has explained to her friend, Trixie. An irresistible urge carries me daily around the apartment perimeter, where I strive to leave a marking scent. This exercise is futile, since a visual inspection of my hindquarters has revealed that my scent glands were removed. Once the urge occurs to set out on a perimeter round, however, I can't relax until it's completed, fruitless or not—a hallmark behavior of instinctual drive.

Other instincts are harder to fathom. After twenty minutes of play, my cozy box calls to me, but a stronger drive keeps me away, a taboo against sleeping during the day, and apparently a recently acquired one, since Joanne told her friend that before the last visit to the vet I used to sleep more than I was awake ... like a normal ferret would. In fact, she has been thinking of taking me back to the vet for a follow-on checkup. She was worried when they told her that they had to keep me overnight, and was relieved when they called the next day for her to come pick me up, but is now concerned that I'm not quite right.

The most perplexing instinct, though, is this one, the one that draws me here at precisely 8:00 each evening, to sit on the dresser in the spare bedroom that Joanne uses for storage. I think about what happened in the course of the day. That's my job. I understand this.

By the way, I suspect other ferrets don't wrestle over the idea of instincts.

∞

I'm worried about Joanne. Every other day or so, she leaves for meetings at the company she works for. Today she came home crying. Not wailing and blowing her nose noisily, but her eyes were puffy, and when she picked me up, she hugged me tight and whispered, "You're always there for me, Rascal." I wanted to ask her what happened, to tell her that she was safe confiding in me, but it came out as a lick on her face, where I detected old blush impregnated with remnant diesel fumes, and the hint of a man's cologne, almost obliterated underneath the overpowering layer of dried, salty tears. This is a man I (apparently) know. His name is Craig. The only other thing I know about him is that when Joanne's not looking, he pushes me slowly away with the side of his foot. He doesn't care for ferrets.

I now know my name as well, and I must face the fact that I am sometimes troublesome.

∞

My dreams are mostly about exploring Joanne's apartment, which indicate that I have been here for some time. I had a strange dream last night, however. In it, I awoke in a place very different from Joanne's apartment—bright lights and the clanking of metal, as though Joanne was rearranging her pots and pans. A man and a woman seemed surprised that I was there. The man had a little pouch under his chin that I imagined might fill with air like a balloon, and then be expelled with a croaking sound. The woman had a scar on her cheek shaped like the motion that Joanne makes when scolding me—she wags her finger back and forth, and then up and down for emphasis. That's all I remember.

Another indication that I have been with Joanne for some time is that she is perplexed by the change in my behavior. She told this to her friend, Trixie. They talk a lot on the phone during the day as Joanne taps away on her laptop at the little desk in the opposite corner from my box. They often talk about Joanne's work—accounts, and budgets, and the short-sighted stupidity of their managers—but just as often about movies and other friends. Joanne worries that maybe I had a stroke or some other dreadful brain ailment, but Trixie told her that it is probably just that I am maturing. Joanne uses a headset, and I have to get close to hear what Trixie is saying. Care is required, since Joanne tolerates my intrusion only so long before reprimanding me and gently removing me, particularly after I walk on the keyboard. As Joanne was carrying me away to the sofa, I heard Trixie say, "It's transference, you know."

"Trixie," Joanne said, "next semester, why don't you take something safe, like history—no, better yet, math."

"I knew about transference before taking psychology. Everybody knows about transference."

"Everybody thinks they know what transference is, you mean. You're talking about Craig."

There it was. My memory was correct.

"Of course," Trixie said. "You're transferring all your fears to Rascal."

"I think Craig had a stroke?"

"Very funny. You know what I mean. He's toxic. Admit it. He's killing you."

"I know. I *know*. You don't understand. He gives me … well, something I need."

"Attention, Joey. He gives you attention. He makes you feel special, but—"

That's all I heard, as Joanne lay me on the sofa cushion and rubbed my stomach before walking back to her desk.

Lying on Joanne's lap, I sometimes watch TV. I learn things, like, for example, that the world is made up of very handsome people who are at the center of things, and other homely people who surround them. I look at Joanne, and I realize that she's probably not somebody who would be at the center on TV. Maybe this is why she likes Craig's attention.

I'm intrigued to learn things. Yet something tells me that the things shown on TV are not new. I protest. They're new to *me*. But there's no response, just the knowledge that I'm wasting my time.

∞

I come to the dresser in the storage room today heavy with regret. I blame it all on the battle I wage with napping. Against napping, actually. A dozen times a day, my little bed in the box calls to me, to snuggle in and snooze. I want to. Irresistibly I am pulled to escape into slumber. But yet I do resist. I have no choice. Any movement towards the box is countered by an overpowering mental leash inhibiting action. The irresistible urge is crushed by uncompromising restraint.

It is a battle that drives me to distraction.

And distraction leads to trouble.

Curiosity is a hallmark of ferrets. I know this because Joanne uses it to justify my blundering annoyances to Trixie, like yesterday when I accidentally did something while exploring the exciting tangle of cords behind her desk that disrupted her conference call. She pulled me out and carried me to the cage, explaining seriously that I had caused her a great deal of embarrassment. She doesn't understand that I understand what she's saying, which is confusing. Why does she talk to me if she thinks I don't understand?

Today, as I do every morning, I woke with the first light. I have come to learn that Joanne sleeps through this, the best time of day, and it is useless to bother her until the sun is up and she's hiding with the cover over her head. I must leave my box and explore, though. This is destiny. Every day it is the same apartment, the same rooms, the same sofa pillows, the smell of the same neighbors' dogs wafting in under the apartment door. Yet I must explore, as if it were all new, as if all the familiar furniture had been replaced with pieces that happened to look exactly like the old. Perhaps I had previously missed some engrossing treasure behind the entertainment shelves, or an amazing treat that Joanne has hidden in the back of one of the kitchen cupboards.

This morning, my investigations shepherded me to Joanne's bedroom. She has the option of closing the door, so the fact that she does not is an open invitation. I know enough to be quiet this early, however. I nosed around her shoes—nothing much interesting, other than the enticing scent of pigeon droppings. From there, I climbed up a wool coat she had left hanging on the standing lamp. Despite the promise of adventure afforded by this wonderful new avenue, the offensive dry-cleaning chemicals were too much to bear, and I had just decided to abandon the wool ascent when I caught sight of the shelf next to me, above her bed. This is normally not accessible, and a split-second decision directed my leap of escape there instead of to the ground. From below, the shelf looks solid. It is not. The unstable platform took me by surprise, and I scratched and scrambled to stay onboard, panic flushing away any care to keep quiet. The slippery polyurethane surface provided nothing for my claws to catch, and I slid away, down, down onto the bed next to the sleeping Joanne.

If my misadventure had been simply that—waking Joanne—I would have escaped with just a scolding, possibly even avoiding internment in the cage. I was not alone on that shelf, however. I had seen the small vase, of course, but until the cursed wool coat provided access, it might as well have been perched on the moon. I knew nothing about it, other than that it looked old—lonely actually, all by itself up there. It is indeed old, its antiquity bestowing value and a favored place above the rest of us transitory possessions. It is in fact a family heirloom, handed down generation after generation, its original source lost in time.

All this I discovered from Joanne's angry rebuke as she carried me off to ferret prison. The vase did not break—she said she would have broken my neck in turn if it had—but it cracked the glass face of her phone. From inside my cage, I watched her poke and slide her finger across the fractured surface. She looked at me and said that it still worked, and that I was a lucky ferret that it did.

I must have looked contrite, for five minutes later, she opened the cage door, reached in, and pulled me to her neck, rubbing her cheek against my fur. She had been crying, her face glistening with tears, which washed me with remorse. I vowed to be more careful in the future. Joanne was so good to me, so patient. I couldn't let this go by without communicating my appreciation. I pulled back so that we were gazing, eye-to-eye. "Dear, Joanne," I said, "I think I hold a deep love for you."

This is what I wanted to say, the words that formed in my brain. I cannot talk, of course. Instead, I placed my paw against her wet cheek, my ferret monologue of affection.

At this, she laughed and cupped my paw in her palm. "Oh, Rascal," she said, her voice sounding nasal through stuffed sinuses. "What would I do without you?"

She lay me gently on the floor. Her laughter subsided into a sardonic grin. "Probably let the bastard talk me into going along with him," she said as she shuffled off back to bed.

I stood watching her. What was she talking about? Was I the bastard? What would I be talking her into? I guessed that it must be Craig. He was making her cry a lot.

I decided that I did not like Craig.

∞

Hello, dresser. It's 8:00. I normally don't talk to an inanimate object like a dresser, but I observe Joanne debating her dinner choices with the refrigerator, and arguing with the TV, and I've decided to try it. Talking to inanimate objects, that is, not arguing with the TV (which is, in its essence, a waste of my time, as I've reluctantly accepted). I can see no obvious benefit resulting from my attempts at communicating with the dresser, however. The words hover there, unabsorbed by the wooden surface until I retrieve them, and then I am left holding them. Perhaps the problem is that my words are not verbalized. Or, maybe Joanne finds value in being left to hold her own words.

I would ask her if I could.

But, dresser, today my destiny has been advanced. At least, this is the sense I have. I feel gratification that I can read. I didn't know I could until I found myself on the kitchen table gazing at a magazine that Joanne had left lying open. I was halfway through an article on making sushi when it suddenly dawned on me what I was doing. At that moment, though, she came in, surprising me. I launched myself into the air, and scampered away. I am not allowed on the table, and being caught there is reason enough to escape, but in this case the dominant impetus was the panic at being caught reading. Ferrets aren't supposed to be able to read, and I feel terror at the thought that Joanne might discover that I can.

Despite the fear that left me shivering in my box, I was filled with a deep sense of satisfaction.

I am a good ferret.

∞

I am a bad ferret, dresser. But I am also a happy ferret. As it turns out, Joanne had taken Trixie's advice a few days ago. This explains why she's been so distraught. She expects that Trixie is right, yet she has been worried that she made a mistake. I did not know until today that Craig is married. Not to Joanne. His wife doesn't know that he's been seeing Joanne. Joanne has known from the beginning that he's married to another woman, which is confusing. I could understand if Joanne were interested in the simple pleasures of sex-play, but this is not the case. She insists that she doesn't care that he's married, yet today she challenged him about it.

But I'm getting ahead of myself.

I was struggling with my sleep taboo, distracting myself by reverse-knitting an old scarf when the doorbell rang, followed immediately with a forceful knock on the door. I do not remember hearing this before, but I knew it was Craig.

So did Joanne, since she called to him to go away even before she looked through the peephole. "There's nothing to say!" she said to the door, as she bit her lower lip.

The familiar, unremembered muffled voice of Craig came from the hallway. "I just want to talk!" he said.

"No, you don't," Joanne said, her forehead resting against the door. "You want to manipulate me."

"That's crazy. That's your friends talking, not you." He was silent a moment while Joanne stared at the floor, unmoving. "Look, I accept that we won't be seeing each other anymore."

Joanne still didn't say anything.

"Okay?" Craig said.

She nodded her head. "Yeah. Okay."

Silence. "I just want to say goodbye," he said.

Joanne stood there, her head propped against the door.

"Okay?" he said.

"You want to change my mind," she finally said.

"I promise. I just want to say goodbye. We owe that much to each other, don't we?"

She took a breath and nodded, then opened the door. "You promised," she said.

He came in quickly, as though the door might snap shut.

This was Craig. So familiar. Physically fit, not too homely. He wouldn't be at the center on TV, but he wouldn't be a caricature oddball friend either. He had confidence, the assured ease that comes with knowing you are in control. "Baby," he said soothingly, grasping her shoulders in his hands and looking into her face.

I watched her eyes soften, and then harden in resolve as she stepped back, out of his grasp. He looked hurt, pained by her rejection. I almost believed it. "Baby," he said, "what's happened to you?"

She looked at him, her brow furrowed. She shook her head. "I've come to my senses, that's what."

"I think it's your friends that have come to you, that's what I think," he said, stepping closer, his palms held open, as if demonstrating that they were empty. "They're jealous, or more likely, misandrous."

At the time, I thought this meant perhaps deformed, but I've come to learn that it means a hatred of men, the opposite of misogyny.

"The problem isn't my friends."

He sighed, an exaggerated patience. "Amy," he concluded.

"Yeah," Joanne said, "your *wife*."

"You know that I don't love her," he said, putting a hand back on her shoulder, which she reached up and slid off.

"You say that," she said, leaning back against the wall, "but you'll never leave her."

"Ah, baby," he crooned, taking a step closer, "you know I would if I could—"

"It's not just the kids, Craig. You know it. I know it."

"Baby! I love you. Haven't I proved that—"

"Craig, I'm through playing the fool. You came to say goodbye, so goodbye."

"Baby, baby," he said as though she'd let him down. "You're forgetting what we have," he said, sliding his hands around her waist.

She grabbed his wrists, and yanked, and for a moment her face tightened in concern before he finally let go of her, stepping back with his hands in the air, as a man does when showing the cop that he has no gun.

"I want you to go, Craig," she said levelly.

"No, baby," he said, stepping towards her again. "You just need some reminding."

"No, you need to leave!" she said, pushing his chest and backing away.

He shook his head, his eyes locked on her with intent. "You know you want it, baby," he said, stepping towards her, and then running when she ran away. She made it to the bedroom, and tried to slam the door shut, but he was there, and kicked it. Hard. With an explosive bang, the door flew open, caved in, where his shoe penetrated the thin veneer surface.

From where I hunkered, I couldn't see them, but I heard Joanne shout, and then her muffled cries, her mouth obviously covered.

I was frozen in place. This was extraordinary. This was the sort of thing I saw on TV. Whatever was telling me that TV was a waste of my time, was clearly wrong. I knew what was happening in that bedroom, and it was making Joanne distraught. No, not distraught—terrified.

That wouldn't do.

I pattered over and looked into the bedroom. All I could see were their feet, twisting and jerking. The bed heaved and swayed as Joanne struggled, her muffled cries becoming desperate. Craig raised himself, one hand still holding Joanne down as he loosened his belt.

No, this wouldn't do at all.

I thought about jumping onto the bed, but what could I do? Nip his leg? He'd just throw me against the wall.

I needed leverage. Height.

I ignored the vile chemicals and scrambled up the wool coat. This time I was ready, and when I jumped onto the shelf, I jammed my claws into the crack between the shelf and the wall, and then scratched and kicked until my hind legs followed. I carefully turned and looked down. Craig had his large hand planted across her mouth. He had pulled open her blouse, and was working at her pants zipper. She stopped beating his head with her fists and stared up at me. I had been scolded once, punished with the cage. For one full second I thought that she was worried that I'd again knock over the precious vase. That was ferret-thinking. She was being raped. The vase was the last thing on her mind.

But not mine.

Even if I got the cage, it didn't matter. The vase was small, but heavy, made of dense ceramic. I placed my head behind it, calculated, and then pushed it hard. I heard a solid thunk, and when I looked down, Craig was swaying, shaking his head, and Joanne yanked his hand away and yelled. The ferret brain took over, and I launched into the air, landing squarely on his head, my claws getting a solid hold in his hair. This time, at least, the ferret brain had done well. He screamed, adding his tortured voice to Joanne's, and reached up to discover what was attacking him. Finding my fur, he grabbed me and pulled, but I hung tight. He yanked hard, ripping his own scalp, but also nearly rupturing my entrails, and I let go. He looked at me, his face blistering red, and, seeing that it was merely Joanne's pet, he threw me like I was a baseball. I would have been killed except for the pile of decorative pillows on the floor that Joanne displays on her bed when she has company.

When I shook off my spinning head and looked, Joanne was screaming and kicking him, so fast and furious, he couldn't do anything except roll off the bed. He stood up, holding his head. "You're fucking crazy, you bitch!" he yelled, and stormed out of the room, pulling up his zipper. Joanne screamed one last time and threw a pillow, a gesture that struck me as symbolic irony.

As the front door of her apartment slammed shut, Joanne broke down, burying her face in her hands to sob. This lasted all of thirty seconds before she suddenly snapped up and scanned the room until she found me lying in the pillows. "Rascal!" she cried as she slid off the bed and ran to me. She knelt down and gently placed her hand on my head, stroking me. "Are you hurt, little buddy?" she said.

Again, she's asking me questions, even though she thinks I don't understand. To assuage her concern, I stepped down from the pillows and stretched ... which actually hurt, but I didn't let on. When I turned back, she was staring at me, a quizzical expression contrasting the tears wetting her cheeks.

Uh, oh.

"Rascal," she said, reaching out to pull me to her, "you did that on purpose." She cupped my chin in her hands and gazed into my eyes. "You knocked down the vase." Her puzzled brow furrowed deeper. "You knew exactly what was going to happen."

At this, I began to tremble, like when she nearly caught me reading, except far worse. The thought of her discovering that I was, apparently, more than a normal ferret was like viewing doom bearing down on me, about to crush me flat. I had to be very careful. I couldn't let this sort of thing happen ever again.

She sat back, pulling me along. "You're pretty smart, you rascal. I'll have to change your name to Hero."

I couldn't take this, and began squirming, trying to get away. At that moment, though, a screech of squealing tires rose from the parking area below, followed an instant later by a grinding crash. Joanne jumped up and ran to the window, and I followed, climbing up on a chair. Below, Craig threw open the door of his car, embedded in the passenger side of another car. A man climbed out of that one, and they started arguing, pointing at the tangled mess of metal and waving their arms. People appeared, watching from a safe distance. The wail of a siren set the appropriate backdrop for the altercation. Craig pushed the man, who took a step back. Craig followed him and pushed again, and this time, the man put his hands up to stop him, at which Craig pulled back and landed a punch on the side of the man's head, causing him to crumble to the ground.

Unfortunately for Craig, the police car had just pulled to a stop. Two policemen got out and ran over, one of them pushing Craig back, while the other knelt next to the fallen man, who waved him off and sat up. We watched the cops talk to some of the bystanders, and then Craig was in handcuffs, the cop pushing down on his head as he maneuvered him into the back of the squad car.

Joanne reached over and stroked my back as we watched the police drive away. A smile spread across her face. "He bought that Jaguar just a month ago," she said.

"Sometimes the universe gets up off its butt and takes out the trash."

I guessed that this was a metaphor. I couldn't see a jaguar, though. Maybe it was in the trunk. I wished I could ask her about that, but the thought of it—somehow asking—set me trembling.

I wasn't sure if I was a bad ferret or a good ferret, but I knew that I was a confused ferret.

Chapter 2

Hello, cardboard box. I've really made a mess of things. I should be on the dresser in Joanne's spare room now. I think it's 8:00, since it's almost dark, and I just heard the church bells, the same ones I normally hear from Joanne's apartment, two floors above me where I now sit.

This box will have to do. Hopefully whatever draws me to Joanne's dresser will accept this. It's sort of like a dresser. It's shaped like, well a box, and it has a flat top. Joanne's spare room is quiet, and I can review the day's events without interruption. Here, I'm constantly startled by cars rushing by out on the street ... and there's always the chance that Duncan will come back.

Whoever's listening, I'm sorry, but if he does, I'll have to run away.

It all started when I realized that I could open the little door next to the hallway closet. No bigger than the laptop that Joanne carries around, it had always intrigued me. Joanne never used it, and, in fact, seemed not to have noticed it. Too low for some sort of tiny closet, it was hinged at the top and seemed specially made for pets. Like me.

Ferrets are, of course, naturally inquisitive, and I felt a thrill when I determined that a little latch that rotated on a bolt was the key to opening it. I could turn the latch with the nails of my paw, but I didn't dare try until Joanne was in the shower. Finding me doing something like this was … well, just not thinkable.

Once unlatched, a heady, wonderful smell of dark dampness welled from the crack that opened at the bottom of the door. I could barely contain myself, and immediately pressed my nose into the opening. Low and behold, that lifted the door up, but it flopped back down as soon as I sat back. I nosed in and pushed it up again, and this time I made sure the swinging door stayed open by letting the bottom slide along my back as I leaned into the fantastic darkness, the irresistible magic of hidden cavities. I realized my mistake too late. By concentrating on maneuvering the door along my back, I lost track of how far I had leaned in. Once I realized that I was dangling over open space, I spun around, but this bounced the door, which deftly tapped me over the edge to fall into unknown blackness.

I tumbled in darkness, falling, falling. I threw out my paws to catch something, but the nails clattered and slid futilely along smooth metal. I seemed to fall for many seconds, but it was only as long as it took to fall two floors into the apartment basement. I landed with a thump that stunned me for a moment. When I regained my senses, I saw that I had landed on a pile of trash—newspapers and paper coffee cups, a spongy landing pad that probably saved my life.

In the dim light that spilled through an open door, I could see that I had plummeted through the ceiling of a small room whose floor and walls were bare cement, coated over the years with tentacles of back mold, like mindless fingers inching along, searching for victims. The overwhelming odor of mildew and traces of robust rat life would normally have stimulated me into heady fascination, to launch into exploration, but I knew that the fall was irreversible. It was a literal fall from grace. I had plummeted down a metal chute, specifically made to transport garbage and stray ferrets in one direction only.

I crawled off the rotting heap and shook each leg, making sure I had no injuries, and then made my way slowly, cautiously out into the lit hallway. This was hardly more comforting than the garbage room, with cracked and broken linoleum flooring and battered drywall, so gouged and marked that bare studs might have been more appealing. I had not understood until now how clean and comfortable Joanne kept her apartment. It was, I now knew, ferret heaven.

And I was banished.

A door slammed, launching me into the air, all four paws leaving the dirty floor. I crouched low, my little heart pattering away like a miniature piston engine. Voices. A man and woman, arguing. He wanted to retrieve a table from storage. She didn't think they had room. I wanted to run, to hide, but I had no idea which way to go. All the doors were closed, other than the garbage room. I could have returned there, but then I would have been trapped.

Suddenly there they were, down the hall. They must have turned a corner. The woman screamed. "A rat!" she squealed. "A *giant* rat!"

I took off in the other direction, my nails skidding on the filthy linoleum. I slid up against a closed door at the end of the hall. Trapped. The man was telling her that I wasn't a rat, but she demanded that he kill me. At that moment, the door before me flew away, open, blinding me with daylight. A man, himself dirty in stained overalls, stood staring at me. The ferret brain took over again, and I scampered out between his legs.

"What in hell's name was that?" I heard him say, but I was already sprinting away—as fast as my short legs could carry me.

I was in an alley—the one, I realized, below Joanne's kitchen window. I would sit on the sill above the sink and gaze down at the kids walking by on their way home from school. It had looked so inviting, so free. The distant shouts of the kids—laughing, accusing, denying—called to me to dance among them, merge myself in the swirling soup of comradery. Then Joanne would come in and shoo me away, leaving the kids' banter echoing through my head.

The woman's demand to kill me swam in my head, and I ducked behind a pile of discarded cardboard boxes, sagging and wilted from days in the rain. The smell of dissolving cardboard glue—distracting—and rotting food residue from nearby trash cans—alarming—filled my nostrils, forcing home the fact that the impression provided from the kitchen window somewhere above me was a lie.

I was shaking. Fear at multiple levels consumed me. The ferret brain was terrified at untested dangers—both already encountered, and possibilities unseen. I was horrified at the seemingly insurmountable dilemma I had created for myself.

I jumped when another door slammed. Silence. I peeked out. It was the door from which I had exited. I tamped down panic, telling myself that there was no useful avenue behind that door. I couldn't very well climb back up the metal chute. On the other hand, the arguing couple obviously lived in one of the apartments. Whatever means they had used to come down, I realized, could potentially have been a way back up. This thought fueled the panic, amplifying the shivering until my teeth chattered.

I froze at the sound of footsteps, the rattling of my teeth seeming loud enough to cause people on the street to pause and turn. The footsteps came closer. Between the sagging folds of the boxes I saw a man shuffling along, an old man, judging by his bent head and leathery hands. He seemed tired, as tired as his once-fine clothes— a tailored sport jacket, now drooping with the weight of years, and matching pants frayed at the bottom where they'd rubbed along the tops of leather shoes, cracked with wear.

I moved to the edge of the box pile and peeked around. This man posed no threat to the ferret brain. It knew instinctively that, even with silly short legs, it could outrun him if needed. The man was carrying what looked like an umbrella, but was actually a small three-legged stool that he unfolded and placed carefully at the edge of the alley before slowly, slowly sitting down. His hands shook, but not from fear, and I noticed that my own shivering had calmed. Anything dangerous would likely accost him first.

He looked right at me, and I jerked back out of view. He had smiled when he'd seen me. He seemed friendly. People were a danger when, like the woman, they wanted to kill me. Or throw me, like Craig. There were other people who visited Joanne. All of them, other than Craig, cooed over me, and petted me until my impatience drove me off their laps. People seemed to be of two categories—those who liked ferrets, and those who didn't. By appearances, this man seemed to be the former.

I peeked around the edge of the box again, and he was staring right at me. I stared back.

"Ah," the man said in a raspy voice, "a ferret. I *thought* you had an awfully short snout for a rat."

He thought a moment, and then reached into a small backpack. "You must be lost," he said, extracting a little brown turd.

It wasn't a turd, but a bone-shaped dog biscuit. I had seen these on TV commercials. One of Joanne's friends had given me one. I suspect that there were other ingredients besides meat—ferrets only digest meat—but there was enough to render it tasty.

And I was hungry. I hadn't eaten in hours (ferrets have a high metabolism).

I took a few steps out from behind my cover, and the old man gave the biscuit a little shake. "Come and get it, fella."

How could a decrepit old man like this hurt me? I approached slowly, the tempting biscuit hovering before me. I stopped a few feet away, or rather, the ferret brain stopped me. *You're also hungry*, I thought, but the animal instinct balked. We struggled for control, and when I won, it was like a rubber band snapping, and I leaped onto the man's lap. He was as surprised as I, but he recovered immediately. "Well, aren't you the friendly one," he rasped, letting me bite the biscuit.

He held on to his end, though. This should have warned me, but now that it was in my mouth, and the taste of animal fat started saliva flowing, I didn't care. I gnawed away, trying to bite off a piece of the tough material. It was like chewing on wood. Only much tastier.

The old man was doing something with his other hand while I struggled to get a purchase on this adversarial meal, a tug-of-war between man and beast. With his free hand, he wrapped a belt around his working forearm as it swayed back and forth with my tugs. Despite his shaking, he managed to feed the end of the belt through the buckle. This all happened right before my eyes. Had I not been distracted with animal needs, I'd like to think I would have seen it coming. As it was, I simply watched as the belt lifted over my head and out of view. When I felt something stiff fall against my back, I froze. I looked up into his eyes, and saw the excitement of anticipation. I finally realized that he had tricked me, and I let go of the biscuit to jump away, but too late—with a jerk, he pulled on the belt, and it locked onto my neck in a choke hold. I fell off his lap, tightening it further. I thrashed in utter panic, which only tightened the belt even more, so that I gasped to get air in my tiny lungs.

"Easy, fella!" the man said, working his end of the belt as though landing a fish. "You're only making it worse."

Like Joanne, he talked to me, even though he couldn't know I understood. But he was right—I was making it worse. I stopped thrashing, the belt clutching me like a cougar's jaws about to snap my neck. I took a step towards the hand holding the belt, giving it slack, and the jaws eased a bit, enough to let air through. I shook my head, letting the slack work into the loop around my neck, and breaths finally came easily. Panic ebbed away.

But I was trapped, a captive. I'd watched people walk their dogs on the sidewalk below, and had thought how pitiful to passively acquiesce to the wills of their master, and now here I was, imprisoned at the end of my own leash.

I had an idea. The old man just wanted a companion. Maybe I could put him off his guard. I jumped up onto his lap and snuggled in, pretending difficulty breathing by constricting my throat so that my breaths wheezed, seeming to come as a struggle. I coughed a little, and snuggled in tighter.

"Well, well," the old man said. "You are the friendliest creature I've had the pleasure to meet. Here, let's loosen that belt."

His shaking fingers fumbled at the buckle next to my neck, and I felt the choke hold give way a little more. He declined to remove it, though, and it would be a struggle to get it off.

I moved on to Plan B. If you can't escape your captor, take your captor along.

I pretended to snuggle into a better position, while maneuvering my head towards the hand holding the bitter end of the belt. All I had to do was give his fingers a nip so he'd let go.

I imagined what I had to do next … and gave an inaudible sigh. I wasn't capable of biting a person, not even a little nip of his hand, a restraint presumably sourced from the same place that drove me to Joanne's dresser each evening.

Plan C.

I chewed the belt, hopefully giving the impression that I thought it was just another treat.

"It's not alive, there, fella. That's not going to make it let go."

I was playing dumb, but he thought I was even dumber. Fine. I played along, growling and shaking the loop of the belt lying in his lap. I made my antics grow frantic, jumping back and forth, creating as much of a bother as possible.

"Calm down!" the old man said. "It used to be a cow, but now it's an inanimate accessory."

I wanted him to think I was totally obsessed with the middle of the belt. With luck, he'd forget to hang on to his end. Suddenly, without a break in my ferret acrobatics, I chomped the belt an inch from his fingers and yanked my head back ... and there was no resistance. He'd lost his grip!

Free! I tried to leap from his lap, but he jerked his knee, retracting my launching pad so that I tumbled to the ground between his feet. I clawed at his pantleg to turn around, and sped away.

I made three feet of freedom.

The jerk on the belt twisted me around, so that my hind legs swung ahead of me in an arc. It hurt! I thought for a moment that my neck had broken, but realized that I would be paralyzed. Or dead.

The old man had stomped on the end of the belt, and he reached down, grabbed it, and reeled me in again. He lifted me high and stared into my face. His watery eyes were searching, looking for something inside my head. "You planned that, didn't you?" he said softly. I stared back. "You played me," he said.

My stomach turned cold. This was bad, maybe as bad as Joanne finding me reading. I had to get away before he discovered more about me. The instinct to hide my intelligence surged through me like a shot of methamphetamine. I exploded into a tornado of twisting and clawing, my feet wheeling freely in the air. The old man hung tight.

"Yo! Duncan!"

The old man's head spun to the side. A younger man was walking towards us from the street, swaying back and forth with each step, his arms swinging, as though pulling him through the air, what I presumed was called a Cool Walk. He wore blue jeans and a leather jacket.

The old man stood up, nodded to him, and put me on the ground, hanging on to the belt.

"What? You got yourself a pet weasel?" the young man said as he stopped before us, combing his fingers through his thick hair.

"It's not a weasel. It's a ferret. You've heard of them?"

"Yeah, I heard of 'em. They're illegal," he said, suddenly frowning and glancing back towards the street.

"You're thinking of California. He's perfectly legal. And valuable."

The young man raised one eyebrow. "Valuable, eh? Maybe to a zoo."

"No. Ferrets are in demand. Highly sought after."

"Forget it, dude. The last thing I want is some animal shitting up my house. You got the money?"

"Of course. But you really should think twice about this. I can give it to you for a tenth the price—"

"Forget it. Cash or no deal."

The old man nodded, resigned, and reached into his pocket to pull out a small manila envelope. The young man reached out, but Duncan pulled the envelope back. "Let's see the merchandise."

The young man laughed. "Merchandise? You think this is, like, the *French Connection?*"

Duncan eyed him. "We could both go to jail."

The young man sobered at this. "You worried? It's a little late to have second thoughts."

Duncan seemed to stare through him. "Twenty years too late," he rasped, a hoarse whisper.

The young man nodded. "I heard you're a doctor."

"*Was* a doctor."

"Yeah. They said they took your license away." He smiled. "Now you gotta' come to guys like me."

"Irony abounds. Have you got the *drugs* or not?"

He emphasized the word, a self-stab at his desperate state.

The young man shrugged. "Would I be here if I didn't?" He grinned. "I guess I would if I was just going to roll you instead."

Duncan looked tired. "Which you're not."

The young man's eyes grew wide—mock aggression. He relaxed and smiled as he took a plastic medicine bottle from his jacket pocket and handed it over.

Duncan pulled reading glasses from his front pocket and read the label. He looked up in alarm. "Oxycodone?" he hissed. "You were supposed get fentanyl!"

The young man shrugged again and reached for the bottle, but Duncan pulled it away. "Good enough?" the young man said.

"Good enough maybe at a quarter the price."

"Suit yourself," the young man said, reaching for the bottle again.

"Here, you son-of-a-bitch," Duncan said, handing him the envelope.

The young man slid the folded wad of money out and glanced through it. "Looks good, dude. See you in a week?"

"I'll call you."

"I need a couple days. Don't wait 'till the last minute. Withdrawal's a bitch, you know."

Duncan stared at him.

"Yeah, yeah," the young man said. "You probably saw your own patients go through it. How'd you put it?" he said laying his hand on Duncan's shoulder. "Irony abounds?"

Duncan knocked his hand off.

"Enjoy," the young man said, turning to go. He stopped and turned back. "Oh, yeah. You got a visitor."

"What do you mean?" Duncan said, frowning.

"You'll see," he said, walking away towards the street.

"Who did you tell!" Duncan yelled, hoarse and desperate.

"Don't worry!" the young man called. "He says he knows you!"

Duncan watched him turn the corner at the street and disappear.

I thought about making a run for it. My captor was obviously distracted and distraught. If I jumped quickly, I might jerk the end of the belt from his hand. I heard Duncan let out a breath, as though he'd been jabbed in the solar plexus. A middle-aged man, maybe thirty-five, had entered the alley. He stared ominously ahead as he walked towards us.

"My God, Schoeman," Duncan whispered.

I thought at first that the man was maybe a shoe salesman.

"You have no business with me!" Duncan called, taking a couple of steps backwards, as though in preparation for running.

"Oh yes I do!" Schoeman called back without breaking stride.

Still hanging on to my belt collar, Duncan picked up the folding stool, shook it closed, and held it high.

"I'm not going to hit you, Duncan," the man said. "What do you take me for?"

He stopped in front of us and folded his arms across his chest. He was handsome and fit. Not in a body-builder way, but as a natural consequence of a job that used all your muscles, like a carpenter, or maybe an oil rig roughneck. If I were Duncan, and, as was obvious, I thought this man held a grudge against me, I would have run away as fast as my wobbly old legs could carry me.

"What do you want from me?" Duncan rasped, still holding his folded stool high. It actually made a decent weapon, since the metal foot pads could slice like a hatchet.

"I just want you to stand there, Duncan. That's all."

"What the hell does that mean?"

"I've been looking for you for months. You covered your trail real well. Have you been hiding from me? Or a whole parade of your patients?"

"I don't have to answer to you. I've done all the answering I need to."

"No, Duncan, not quite. You have one last person to answer to."

The color leached from Duncan's face. "You received a substantial settlement and got me disbarred! Do you want my blood as well?"

Schoeman looked at him, as though considering it. "Most of the settlement went to lawyer fees. The rest for physical therapy." He frowned and shook his head. "Ten years ago I could have hurt you, Duncan. I wanted to. I've gotten past that, for my own sake. Seeking revenge means giving up your life. I've taken my life back. I'm not here for revenge, Duncan."

The old man stood up straight. "Then, what?"

I sensed that Duncan knew exactly for what, but clung to the idea that it wasn't real until spoken.

"Honey!" the man called over his shoulder. "You can come now."

Duncan shook his head, slowly at first, and then faster, as though rejecting what was about to happen.

What happened was that a pretty girl, maybe seventeen, hobbled around the corner. Below her skirt, she wore braces on both legs, and leaned heavily on a cane. Her knees were odd, outsized, like a python that swallowed a whole pig. She gazed steadily ahead, the look of someone who has been wading all her years through curious stares and frowns of pity.

Duncan took a step backwards, but Schoeman grabbed his arm. "You owe her this," he said softly.

Duncan opened his mouth to protest, but clamped it shut as the girl arrived, stopping ten feet away, leaning on her cane. Her brow furrowed a little as she studied Duncan, as though unsure whether this was the man she expected.

Still holding Duncan's arm, Schoeman said, "Tell her what happened."

"She knows," Duncan said. "She sat through the trial."

"She was seven. I want her to hear it from you."

Duncan looked at her. He opened his mouth again, but shut it, turning his eyes back to the man. "If you're out to punish me, to dig out old wounds—" he shook his head. "Looks like you get your revenge after all."

"I said this wasn't about revenge," Schoeman said. "You damaged my beautiful little girl—" He stopped and closed his eyes, tears squeezing through the cracks. "This is about the damage done by her mother," he said opening them again.

Duncan looked at him in surprise. He shook his head, not understanding.

"She refused to accept that Tiffany was crippled," Schoeman said. "She wouldn't even say the word. She wanted a perfect little daughter. She was convinced that Tiffany just wasn't trying. She's gone now, but only after years of hounding her, never letting up. She kept at it until … until—"

He broke, burying his face in his hands. Sobs broke the silence of the alley with propulsive gasps of air.

Tiffany blinked slowly, as though in a trance, and held out her arms, palms up. The wrist scars were like perforated demarcations, where you'd rub your fingernail to detach the hands.

Duncan stared, seeming mesmerized himself. "What do you want from me?" he asked in a voice coming from somewhere far away.

"I told you," Schoeman said, forcing aside his grief and wiping snot away with his sleeve. "I want her to hear it from you."

"Why?" Duncan said, swinging his eyes to look at him.

"She needs to understand—to believe—that it wasn't her fault."

"She knows that. She doesn't need me to tell her—"

"Stop!"

The silence in the alley was a cushion, insulating them from the sound of traffic out on the street.

"You have to tell her," Schoeman said. "She needs to hear it from you, the person who ruined her life. Tell her."

Duncan sighed and took a breath, as though finally deciding that this was all silly. "Fine. Tiffany, it was I who ruined your life." He turned to Schoeman. "Can I go now?"

Tiffany's father stood, clenching his fists, his face nearly bursting with red fury.

I knew that Duncan was about to get punched. Maybe kicked when he went down. Part of me wanted to warn him, but another part just wanted the man to get it over with.

"I had Lyme disease," Tiffany said in a monotone.

Duncan stiffened, and her father looked at her, concerned.

"You told us it was multiple sclerosis," she said, as though reading a report to her class. "Daddy wanted a second opinion, but you convinced him that it would be a waste of his money. Instead, you prescribed Fingolimod, which suppressed my lymphocytes. This can be good for people who actually have MS, but is exactly the wrong thing for Lyme disease, since it allows the bacteria to grow. Mine progressed so fast, I developed crippling damage before it could be stopped."

The cushion of silence was smothering.

"I … I'm so sorry," Duncan whispered, all sign of frivolity evaporated. "I made a mistake."

"A mistake wouldn't have gotten you dis-barred," Tiffany said. Her voice gained strength in inverse proportion to Duncan's diminution. "You needed money to support your habit. The drug company representative—"

"That was exaggerated!" Duncan pleaded.

Tiffany continued, speaking louder, climbing over top of his objection. "The representative was giving you money under the table to push a new form of this drug—"

"That was just a coincidence!"

Tiffany was shouting now. "You ruined me!"

The cushion hovered over them, trembling. Tiffany burst it wide open as she screamed and fell on him. Her cane clattered to the pavement as she pounded his chest with her small, girl fists. He shuffled backwards, and she tried to follow, but stumbled so that she ended up with her arms wrapped around his neck, sobbing into his stained, wrinkled shirt. Duncan stood, frozen, blinking into her hair.

Her father stepped in, placed a hand on each arm, and urged her back. Wrapping his arm around her shoulders, he led her, limping, away. She stopped, turned, and pointed. Schoeman came back and picked up her cane. He brought it to her, whispered something into her ear, and returned to face Duncan. He jabbed a finger into the wrinkled shirt, wet with his daughter's tears. "You took a solemn oath to do no harm," he said quietly, steadily. "I hope you're not religious, because that's a broken promise you'll be explaining in hell."

He removed his finger, turned, and walked back to his daughter.

I heard a whistle, like the first steam finding the strength to lift the kettle cap. It was Duncan, his face contorted, twisted in excruciating emotion, and the whistle was a suppressed scream. He still held his stool, and he raised it again, his hatchet poised for deadly action.

He had dropped the belt. An actual ferret would have been long gone, but I am cursed to understand. The old doctor staggered forward, advancing towards the backs of the unsuspecting father and daughter. I did the only thing I could—I ran to catch up and bite his ankle. I caught him easily, and opened my little jaws with their sharp little teeth ... but I couldn't. I am not able to bite a person. Ridiculous as it seems now, I launched myself up and grabbed his pantleg, as though climbing a tree, thinking that—somehow—I was going to topple him. The burden was as nothing to him, and he barely missed a stride.

My nails are sharp as well, however. I don't think I can deliberately claw a person, but I didn't realize that when I grabbed his pants my talons would penetrate the flesh underneath.

The murderous old man howled in pain, and Schoeman whirled around, caught the middle of the stool hatchet in his palm, tearing it away. He tossed it so that it clattered across the filthy pavement. He looked down at me curiously, still attached like a tree frog as Duncan wailed in irrepressible anguish. The old man reached down to pull me off, but Tiffany's father stopped him with a hand on his shoulder. Instead, he reached towards me.

The ferret brain took over. I leaped away, and ran off.

From the other end of the alley I stopped and looked back. If I never find my way back to Joanne, this man could have been my haven. But Duncan stood between us. The discredited doctor could easily convince Schoeman that I belonged to him.

I turned and slunk away around the corner.

So now, here I sit, a lost and lonely ferret as darkness falls on a world I know only from TV, and which I fear is far more complicated than my little ferret brain had suspected.

Chapter 3

Hello, cardboard box. Night two in the alley begins. I am an emotional contradiction. The ferret brain, following its crepuscular behavior, feels invigorated, knowing that the sun is setting. The me is surrounded by ill-defined dangers, perhaps worse than those known. The unease has even infiltrated my dreams. Last night, following another strange dream where I woke up in the brightly-lit room, I was back with Duncan, Tiffany, and her father. This time, when I ran to jump onto Duncan's leg, he suddenly stopped, turned, and swung his stool at me. The sharp edge caught me in the stomach, and I knew that it was a mortal blow. I woke trembling with terror.

My hunger, all-consuming until a half hour ago, is finally abated, but at a cost that I will bear as long as my memory holds. I was ready to eat the cardboard of this box, or perhaps my own paw, when I heard a rustling. The ferret brain held me frozen, waiting. I caught motion out of the corner of my eye. I slowly turned my head, and saw black fur, a small rat. I was curious, as I had been mistaken for one. The ferret brain, however, was excited. A slight breeze funneled down the alley, and I caught the scent of animal. This meant that the rat wouldn't smell me. The little fool scurried along the wall, and then along the bottom of the box, right below me. My association with food is my bowl that sits in Joanne's kitchen. Despite my gnawing hunger, this rodent was just that, an animal. Had I taken a moment to think about it, I would have realized that rats are ferret prey.

The ferret brain didn't have to think about that. It saw food and pounced. One moment I was sitting, still as stone, and the next, I was on the pavement with a squealing rat under my front paws. The tiny black eyes, like inverted stars, stared up at me in utter terror for a brief second before the ferret crunched its neck, leaking the life from them. I was stunned, barely conscious as each tearing, crunching bite slowly filled my stomach with the sustenance of raw animal.

As horrendous as the experience was, I would be a hypocrite to condemn the ferret, since I sit here now grateful for the extended lease on life that the rat's sacrifice has provided.

∞

Hello, dresser. I can truthfully say that again. I just wish it was Joanne's dresser. Not that I am resentful of Trey. After all, he probably saved my life. Still, I wish I was back in Joanne's apartment instead of here. In a cage. A carrier, actually. A dog carrier, at that. It's humiliating.

I should explain.

After two nights in the alley, martyring a rat, I decided that desperate circumstances require desperate measures, as somebody said. If there was an alley outside Joanne's apartment, there had to be a front door to the building somewhere else, and she had to leave sometime—for work, or shopping, or doing things with her friends, what she calls "going out"—and perhaps I could catch her. I slunk slowly, cautiously along the wall to the end of the alley that opened to the street. Someone walked by, and I sank down and back, crouching against the wall, becoming ferret-invisible. The footsteps faded, and I looked out. I saw a sign at the intersection indicating that this was Maple Street, and I uttered a little squeal of delight, which scared me, and I crouched back again. I knew from her mail that Joanne's address was Maple Street.

I peeked out, and crouched back yet again as people approached. I hovered like this, in and out, for maybe fifteen minutes before the street was empty of pedestrians, at least as far as I could see from my position a few inches above the pavement. Taking a deep breath, my little heart pattering away like the sound the perforated plastic tab makes when Joanne rips it away from the prepared food, I slithered around the corner. This was ridiculously dangerous. I decided that I was out of my mind. On the other hand, I wouldn't have known how to judge a sane ferret.

I didn't know where I was going, only hoping that I'd recognize the entrance ... and then find a place to hide. I was definitely out of my mind.

I came to a short flight of three steps, and at that moment, a door at the top flew open. I believe my heart stopped, and I froze. The man was frowning at his phone as he trotted down the stairs and away. The door above was slowly closing. I had about one second to decide. I had no idea if this was Joanne's entrance. Instead of deciding, I let fate take responsibility, and went for it. My feet barely tapped the cement steps, but the door was almost shut, the opening not nearly large enough. Since I was out of my mind anyway, I dove through. Fortunately, ferrets have short tails.

I was in a little lobby, nothing more than a space between two sets of doors. Fate had arranged for the management to place a large potted plant in the corner, and I crawled behind this. I couldn't see my other end, and guessed that my rear showed, so I lay flat, hoping my furry bottom would look like some remnant of a dog's lost chew toy.

The inner door opened. I heard the distinctive click-click of stiletto heels. Joanne normally wore these only when she went out at night, but I couldn't take a chance. I scrambled to move out, but caught only a flash of skirt as the outer door closed. I didn't recognize the color, but could I honestly say that I had seen all her clothes?

I backed myself again behind the pot. This could take a long time. I could starve. Joanne had to come through sometime. Even if she didn't go to the office, she went out every day, if just for a walk.

I simply had to be patient.

This was assuming, of course, that I'd even gotten the right entrance.

The outer door opened. I knew immediately that this was not Joanne, and I didn't move. This was a man. The little foyer suddenly reeked of stale cigar, and a rattling, throaty cough confirmed that this wasn't my sweet owner.

Lie still. Let him pass.

But he didn't. The little space was quiet. What was he doing? I daren't move to look.

"What the hell?" he muttered, and coughed again, this time the rattling phlegm swooping closer. Acrid cigar mixed with yeasty beer breath washed over me, and suddenly my rear end was rising, grasped by strong fingers.

The ferret brain went berserk, and I twisted and thrashed, which evoked a "Jee-sus Kee-riest!" from the man as he gripped me harder while I soared upside down into the air.

"What in God's name …?" he said loudly, holding me up to peer at me.

I needed to bite him. The ferret brain was frantic to bite him. I couldn't, of course. Even the ferret brain's adrenaline-fueled panic couldn't convince the little jaws to clamp the man's wrist.

He shrugged and dropped me into a bucket he was carrying. I leapt up, and my head smacked into a lid coming down, and then I was in darkness. I slipped and stumbled on smooth metal objects, probably tools the man had been carrying in the bucket. They rolled and rattled about as the bucket swayed, and one of my paws caught painfully between two shifting cylinders. I decided I had better just lie still for now.

Nice joke, fate.

Amid my panic, I hadn't gotten a glimpse of the man's face, but I recognized his smell. He had come to fix Joanne's toilet one afternoon. Perhaps he was on his way to her apartment again! It seemed unlikely, as there must be over a dozen units in the building, but hope springs eternal, as somebody said. Come to think of it, I'm not sure if that aphorism is supposed to be encouraging, or belittling.

The bucket rattled and swayed as I tried my best to stay on top of the rolling metal logs. At one point he set it down, and I considered pushing up the lid to make a run for it, but we were up and away again before I could even decide. He stopped to talk to someone, and I became excited when I heard a woman's voice. My heart sank, though, when she pointed out that he had grease on his hands, and that he was likely to get it all over the doorknobs. Joanne would never be so rude. Also, the woman sounded to be octogenarian.

A collision sent me and the tools flying and I curled into a ball in hopes of saving extremities. A jolting bump, and motion stopped. He had set us down. My ears rang from the din of clanking metal, but I became aware that he was talking to somebody. "Dad," a younger man said, "you're supposed to be resting today."

"I'll rest when I'm dead, Trey," my captor replied.

"Which means that you're going to be resting soon either way—I'd just rather you be alive when you do."

"You lay down," the older man philosophized, "and you're half way to the grave."

"That's your own father talking. This isn't the Great Depression, you know."

"God made man to work."

"Come on, Dad. That's propaganda invented by people who reap the benefits of your labor."

"You're one to talk. You wouldn't know a crescent wrench from a monkey wrench."

"That's not fair. You never wanted me to follow your footsteps. It was either college, or hit the road."

"True, true. I never figured you'd make money betting with other people's money, though. Hell, you bet on failure. You're rooting that companies hit the toilet."

"Dad, we've been over this. Hedge funds play an important role in finance. It's risk management. We provide stability in uneven markets."

"You make money when somebody else loses their shirt."

"That's called a financial market, Dad."

"That's called whistling with the Devil—sorry, son. I know you're an honest kid. Good at what you do, too, apparently. They gave you a bonus."

"How do you know that?"

"Your sister. She saw your post on Facebook. Isn't that a little dangerous?"

"What do you mean?"

"I don't know. Advertising the fact."

"It's not like I posted the amount or anything. Besides, everybody gets a bonus this time of year."

"Still. There's a lot of rats out there—hey, speaking of rats, I got one of my own today."

"What are you talking about?"

"Right out there in your lobby, a huge rat."

"A rat? In broad daylight? You kidding?"

"Nope. It was hiding behind the ficus. If the manager won't pay my overtime, I'll just start casually showing this to your neighbors."

I jumped when thunder rumbled from above. The father must have tapped the lid.

"Dad, don't be stupid. Benjamin's stubborn. You know that. He'll just give you more trouble. What are you going to do with it? I mean, really?"

"Don't know. To tell you the truth, it may not be a rat at all. It *looks* like a rat, but then again, it doesn't. Maybe it's one of those lab rats—genetically modified."

"Let me see. It's in this bucket?"

"It'll jump out if you open the lid."

"It's that big?"

"I told you, it's huge. May not be a rat."

"Here, maybe we can get it into Trump's carry cage."

"Your dog won't mind?"

"He'll have no choice. Here, hold these books along the sides as I raise the lid."

"What if he gets away?"

"I guess Trump will take care of him."

"I don't know. This fella' could give your dog a run for his money."

"It won't get away. Come on, hold the books. Steady …"

The bucket shook a little, and then a little popping sound let a blast of light inside. A man's eye peered through the crack. "I think I see fur," Trey said.

"He'd be a Houdini rat if you didn't."

"Okay, here goes …"

The lid slowly lifted, and sure enough, book covers blocked each side. Directly in front of me was the opening of a cage very similar to mine, the one to which I was banished when Joanne had had enough of me. Above the cage was the face of Trey, a little pudgy, but not in a doughy way, more handsomeness slightly inflated.

He looked at me expectantly, and I looked back skeptically. Did he expect a ferret to voluntarily jump into a cage with a stranger hovering above?

"Dad!" he said, "That's not a rat, it's a ferret!"

"I told you it wasn't a rat," the father said.

"It must be somebody's pet."

That's all I needed. I leapt, caught the lip of the cage, and crawled inside. Exiting the blackness of a bucket filled with mincing metal, this was essentially escape.

"You want him, Dad?" Trey said, closing the door.

"Nah. Hardly any meat on him at all."

"Dad! He's a pet, not a—"

"I'm kidding! Son, you gotta get out more."

"Right, Dad. I'm the one who thinks social media is some kind of venereal disease."

"It is. In a way. What would I do with a ferret? I'd forget to feed it, and then it would chew my hand off while I was asleep."

"You can just say you don't want it."

"I don't want it."

Trey looked at me and sighed. "I'll post some notices. Maybe it belongs to somebody in the building."

I could have kissed the full, handsome face. Instead, I did a little hop-skip and turn for joy, until I whacked my head against a brace.

The father laughed. "Seems like he understood you."

I froze. The fur on the back of my neck went stiff. Trey didn't respond, as though he hadn't heard his father. Instead, he tapped the cage lightly with the tip of his finger. "You okay, fella?"

My panic eased. He wasn't really talking to me. I was getting used to this. Trey didn't suspect that there was a third sentient intelligence in the room.

"I'll leave so you and the big rat can get acquainted," the father said. "Mrs. Lubbard is expecting a new commode."

"It's a ferret—Benjamin okayed a whole new toilet?"

"Nope. That's what she's expecting. She's getting a new flapper. See you on Sunday?"

"Huh? Yeah, sure. Around one o'clock," he said, his face right up to the cage.

Trey was staring at me, which made me nervous. Maybe he suspected something after all. "You hungry?" he said.

Maybe it was a trap, to see if I responded, like when Germans during WWII suspected an American spy, and would suddenly ask something in English.

But I was hungry. Very. Survival instinct is powerful, and the fact that I didn't react testified to the strength of my true-colors inhibition.

"Trump won't mind sharing," Trey said, and went to a cupboard in the little kitchen area. I heard the click and swish of a pop-seal, and the gorgeous aroma of factory-processed meat filled the apartment. My stomach rumbled with anticipation.

From behind a door—presumably the bedroom—came the sudden yapping of an excited dog, apparently Trump. He detected it as well.

Trey opened the door to my cage just enough to slip in the open can. Pushing aside caution and pleasantries, I buried my snout in the juicy portion. Three full swallows hustled each other down my gullet before I recognized the problem. The "meat" was flavor only. A great majority of the can's contents was grain. I looked up at Trey, radiating indignant psychic energy. He smiled back. "Good, huh?" he said, and turned away.

I looked down at the messy contents, and dove back in. The grain carbohydrates would pass unprocessed through my gut, but the juice must contain meat fat, which provide some amount of sustenance.

Plus, it tasted wonderful.

I was half way through when Trey opened the bedroom door and let loose the demon. Trump, it turns out, is the most angry, obstinate, irritable—and irritating—creature on the face of the Earth. At least in my limited experience. I guess him to be a miniature poodle, although that is by breed only—his soul is pure

Beelzebub. He scanned the room, howled holy terror, and shot like a loosed arrow up a chair, and onto the table next to where the cage lay. Alternating death-promising growls and ear-piercing yelps, he threw himself at the cage, as though convinced that the mesh was made of wet spaghetti. The fact that it wasn't, seemed only to enrage him more.

His viciousness had startled me, and it reflexively pushed me to huddle against the far side. I knew he couldn't get to me inside the cage, though, and I was determined to just ignore him, which, with luck, would drive him into an even greater frothing frenzy, and with more luck, cause cardiac arrest.

The ferret brain didn't share the same intellectual conclusion, however, and opened my mouth wide and hissed. This gave the demon a moment's pause, only to send him into greater hysterics.

I had to admit, the ferret brain had achieved the desired effect in shorter time.

Trey ran over. "Trump! Down boy!" he said, picking up the little banshee. "This guy's our guest. Be nice." The miniature monster jerked and squirmed as Trey put him on the floor, and as soon as he let go, the weaponized mouth with a dog attached was back at the cage in an instant.

"Okay," Trey said, grabbing him again. "It's solitary confinement for bad behavior." He tossed the brat underhand, like a softball, into the bedroom and closed the door. To me, he said, "My apologies."

"My condolences to you," I said in return, but of course, the words were only in my head.

A tinkling sound issued from his pocket, and he pulled out his phone. "Hey, Desmond," he said, putting it to his ear, "it's about time. Hold on." He flipped open a laptop sitting on the table. "Okay, shoot." He typed as he listened.

I could see the laptop screen. The image seemed crude compared to the colorful gala websites that Joanne visited. A bland, gray pattern filled the screen, with a window box in the middle into which he typed. The display suddenly changed to a cartoon human skull, with a white character entry area inside the mouth. "Okay," Trey said, "I've launched the app."

He set the phone on the table, and a voice spoke from it. "It's waiting for the password?"

"I guess," Trey said. "It looks awfully primitive."

"This is just the portal software, sort of like your browser."

"Yeah. I don't know. I don't like it. Why can't I just use my regular browser?"

"It uses proprietary packet transaction formats. Your browser wouldn't know how to talk to it."

"Is that necessary?"

"That's why they call it the dark web, dummy. They don't want any old fool to stumble on them."

"Yeah. I know. It's just ... you sure this isn't going to, like infect my computer?"

"Look, Trey, I didn't have to bring you in. If you've got cold feet, then now's the time to back out. After contact, there's no turning back, you know. I told you that."

"Yeah, yeah. It's a big decision, Desmond. I don't understand why you aren't nervous."

"I was. I thought it was a scam at first."

Trey laughed nervously. "Gee, I wonder why?"

"Look, I know it sounds crazy. If you have doubts—in fact, Trey, maybe you should just forget about it."

"And miss the chance of a lifetime?" He laughed again. "I guess the keyword there is 'lifetime.'"

"I'm not the one that needs convincing. I like the idea of a lifetime that has no limits. To me it's worth the risk—hell, *any* risk."

Trey shook his head. "It's just so … bizarre. Immortality. It's science fiction."

"You're right, Trey. Forget it. Remember, you promised not to talk about this. Not to anybody. Not even to me after this."

Trey sat back, entwined his fingers behind his head, and stared at the ceiling.

"You there?" came the voice from the phone.

"I'm ready, Desmond. Let's do it."

"You positive? It's not a game."

"Yeah. Positive. Give me the password."

Desmond, whoever he was, slowly conveyed a series of random letters, which Trey carefully typed in. He lifted his finger, paused, and brought it down on the enter key. The screen suddenly changed to an intricate multi-colored, realistically three-dimensional matrix.

"Pretty snazzy," Trey said. "Uh, it's asking for another password. Hey! It says, 'The FBI has determined that access to this site constitutes a federal treason offense under US Code Title 18, paragraphs 2384 and 2389.' Desmond! What the hell?"

"Keep your shirt on. That's just to scare away the insecure dabblers … like you."

"It's not true? I mean that just accessing this site is, like, a federal crime?"

"Listen, friend, the FBI stays clear of this area. It's out of their league."

"You're kidding."

"They made me promise not to talk about this until you were committed. The government's always been doing deep, dark stuff—at least after WWII. The FBI knows there's areas that are off limits."

"So, like, the president's in on it?"

"What do you think?"

"You're serious? The *president* has signed up for immortality?"

"You seriously think he *wouldn't?*"

"Good point." He took a breath. "Okay. What's the second password."

"Enter."

"Just the enter key?"

"Like I said, this screen is just a dummy warning."

Trey hit the key, and another window appeared with multiple data entry boxes. "It says to make sure my laptop camera is enabled. Really?"

"Have you disabled it?"

"No."

"Then it doesn't matter."

"What do you mean?"

"They've already got video of you."

"Hey! You said they wouldn't infect my computer!"

"Careful, friend. The video includes audio, you know."

"Ah, shit!" Trey muttered. "What am I getting myself into?"

He began filling in the entry boxes. "Jesus!" he said. "They want my street address and social security number."

"You think that information isn't already plastered around the world in a hundred different hacked data bases?"

Trey shrugged and finished the entries. "I'm done," he said.

"Then hit 'submit.'"

"Huh."

"What?"

"I never thought about the other meaning of that word."

"What word?"

"Submit. Most people think, 'I'm allowing the information to now be sent,' but it could also mean, 'I am giving myself up to you.'"

"Trey."

"What?"

"Did you hit the key?"

"Uh, now I did—hey! The screen went blank!"

"So?"

"Don't I get an acknowledgement or something?"

"Your acknowledgement is on the way."

"By mail? That seems an unlikely way to—"

"Not by mail. You'll find out. I gotta go."

"Wait! Desmond! ... You there? Crap." He looked at me. "Do ferrets think about immortality?"

"Now they do," I said, but he didn't hear.

∞

I returned from deep musing to the demon barking in the bedroom. I'd lost track of time wondering if this is why I'm here—to discover the secret of immortality. I had no idea how long it had been. I heard the doorbell, the reason the monster was clawing at the other side of the door.

"Quiet!" Trey called as he went to the apartment door and opened it. He stepped back quickly as a man in a plain suit and carrying a manila envelope walked past him, glancing around. "Excuse me," Trey said, "you can't just walk right in—"

"Is anybody in the bedroom?" the man asked, as though he hadn't heard Trey. His suit looked like it had served up years of loyal duty. The black shoes shone with polish.

"Uh, no," Trey said. "Listen, who are you—?"

"Are you Trey Rothrauf?"

"Yeah, but you need to—"

"Ewen," the man said, reaching into his inside jacket pocket. "Daniel Ewen." He pulled out a black leather ID case, flipped it open, and held it up for Trey to see.

"FBI?" Trey squeaked.

Ewen put the badge away. "You visited a restricted website a couple of hours ago."

Trey's face was white. He blinked at regular intervals, like the ticking of a clock. "Yes. But I haven't—"

"Who gave you the password?"

Trey stared at him, and his lips pressed together to form a perfect line. "I want to see a lawyer."

"You have that right, but I can tell you, it will go a lot easier for you if you just cooperate. I can forget you tried to contact the organization if you give me that name. Otherwise, I'm going to have to take you in."

I thought that Trey was going to cry. His mouth twitched. He opened it to say something, but closed it again. He stared at the floor, and then looked at Ewen. "I want a lawyer."

Ewen looked at him, and then the corner of his mouth turned up for just a moment. "Relax, Trey. You passed."

"Passed? What do you mean?"

Ewen took off his jacket and hung it over the back of a chair. He looked at me. "Unusual pet."

"Um, it's not mine—what do you mean 'I passed'?"

"Trey, I'm not with the FBI. I'm with the organization."

Trey's eyes went wide. "You tricked me!"

Ewen shrugged. "Like I said, you passed. I'm not sure you understand just how critical caution is at this point."

"To, uh, trust me?"

"Yes. We have to be sure you will maintain utter secrecy. From everyone—from family, friends, even the police."

"Desmond said that the organization was outside the FBI's—"

"Desmond?"

"Yeah, Desmond. My friend who—"

Ewen was watching him with raised eyebrows.

"Right," Trey said. "I see. Sorry. I'm still adjusting here."

Ewen nodded. "So, who's Desmond?"

Trey shook his head. "Nobody. I made him up."

Ewen nodded approval. "That's better."

Trey took a breath. "Hey, that was quick. I logged in, like, only a couple of hours ago—"

"The countdown starts once we know someone has discovered us."

"Countdown … towards what?"

"Confirmation."

"Of what?"

"A viable subject."

"I'm the viable subject?"

"We'll see."

"Whether I'm viable?"

Ewen's shoulders raised a bare perceptible amount.

"Subject," Trey said. "It makes it sound as though it's an experiment."

"It is, in a way. The process hasn't been tested on a wider range of humans."

"The, uh, process—immortality?"

Ewen's brows sank together.

"Uh, oh," Trey said. "Des—I mean somebody told me that's what it's all about. Immortality, I mean. Um. what *is* it about?"

"Basically, what you heard. We don't think of it in terms of that. Immortality implies that you can't die. After the process, you certainly can die. You could kill yourself if you wanted. The process simply manipulates your genes so that your cells stop aging. We don't really know how long you'd live short of accidental or purposeful death."

"I see. Uh, what's the longest anybody's lived after the, um, process?"

"We've been administering the process for seventeen years."

"Oh. Not long enough to really know anything—"

"The third subject was seventy-eight years old."

"Really? He's, uh, still alive?"

"It's a 'she,' and she works at Walmart. She had to change jobs once, since her co-workers were beginning to notice that she wasn't aging."

"Really?"

"I'm not here to sell you. Understand, it's up to *you* to sell *me*."

"Right. Hey! What if I'm not able to. Sell you."

Ewen raised his shoulders. "You don't get the treatment."

"That's it? I'm just not accepted?"

"And you don't tell anybody about us."

"Of course. Um, but, like, you know, what's to stop me? I mean, if you've already rejected me, it's not like I have anything to lose—"

"Yes, you do."

"What? Like a deposit, or something?"

"There is a token deposit, but that's not the purpose. In fact, you get the deposit back as soon as you sign the NDA and commitment paperwork."

"That's what's in the envelope?"

Ewen nodded.

"Why all the super secrecy?" Trey said.

"What do you think would happen if this was generally known?"

"Yeah. I see. The entire world would be clamoring for it."

"We've never done this before—gone outside the organization. The scope of the experiment is far larger than anything we've ever tried. We need volunteers. It's that simple."

"What's the deposit for?"

"It's a legal binder."

"For what?"

Ewen smiled for the first time. "There's nothing like an exchange of fees to legally bind an association."

"Sorry, I still don't get it."

"Look, we need you to keep quiet. You don't? We discredit you. The whole thing sounds far-fetched, after all. It will be easy to establish that you are delusional. You see, the payment is membership to a non-profit organization—not ours—whose charter maintains that the government has secretly constructed a giant laser on the far side of the moon, and that they are in contact with aliens."

"I see. This organization, I'm guessing that you actually created it."

Ewen nodded. "It has over three hundred members."

"Yikes! That many rejects?"

Ewen smiled again. "Almost all of the members are bona fide crackpots—found the website all on their own. It's a real nut-case club, with yearly conventions. This last February it was held in Tallahassee. T-shirts sold out the first morning."

"This is, like, blackmail."

"More like insurance."

"Yeah, like Mafia insurance."

"Look, *you* contacted *us*. I can walk out the door, and we can forget the whole thing." He considered, and shook his head. "In fact, I think we're done here," he said as he put his jacket back on and walked to the door.

Trey ran and cut him off. "Wait! I'm sorry. I'm just being careful. You said it yourself, the whole thing sounds far-fetched."

Ewen studied him. He glanced at me. "Not your pet, you say?"

"No. No! I have a dog. A very normal dog."

Ewen looked at Trey, and nodded. "What the hell," he said as he turned back. "No skin off our backs." He held out the envelope. "Look it over. Give me a call when you're ready to sign."

Trey tried to take it, but Ewen held on. "Not so fast. I can't leave these without that insurance."

"The membership payment?"

"That's right."

It was Trey's turn to look skeptical. "How much are we talking about?"

"Forty dollars."

"Ah," Trey said, relieved. "Hang on, I'll get my checkbook—"

"No."

"No?"

"I'm not part of the nut-case club. Remember?"

Trey shrugged. "How do I pay then?"

"The same as all the other Looney Tune members."

"Online?"

"Bingo. The site's called Truth Platoon—I didn't come up with that one."

"Um, okay," Trey said as he logged onto his laptop.

Ewen looked at his phone as it beeped.

"You need to take that?" Trey asked, while he typed in the search words.

"No," he said, tapping the screen. "I'll call back. You find the site yet?"

Trey pointed at the display. "They don't leave much doubt." The screen showed the title, on top of a crude drawing of the moon, with a green beam of light shooting off into the stars.

"Like I said, I didn't come up with it."

Trey jumped at the sound of the doorbell. "Probably some soccer kid begging for a donation," he said as he worked the mouse, finding his way to the admission page.

The doorbell rang again, three insistent jabs. "Christ," Trey muttered as he went to the door.

The man wore a sweater-vest under a sports coat. He looked like a minister. "You're Trey, right?" he said.

"Yeah," Trey said cautiously. "Why?"

"Hi," he said, holding out his hand. "I'm Bob—Bob Cranston, a neighbor. Can I bother you to help me a minute?"

"I'm, um, in the middle of something," Trey said, reluctantly shaking Bob's hand.

The man glanced at Ewen and frowned. "It'll take just a minute. It affects everybody in the building."

Trey sighed. "Fine. You on this floor?"

"It's downstairs."

"Sorry," Trey said, turning to Ewen. "I'll be right back."

Ewen scowled. "I'm on a schedule."

"Three minutes," Mister Rogers said, throwing Ewen a hard look. "That's all I need."

Trey paused, conflicted. "Really?" he said to Bob.

"Guaranteed. Less than three minutes if we hurry."

Trey sighed. "I'll be right back," he said, closing the door behind him as he walked out.

Ewen looked at the door, then reached into his pocket and pulled out a small black stick, like a flattened version of one of Joanne's lipstick tubes. Going to the laptop, he inserted the stick into the side, waited, then tapped away at the keyboard. He watched as a black window appeared and a storm of white text slid up, pausing occasionally as the laptop whirred into a higher pitch. The window disappeared, and Ewen detached the little stick and poked at his phone with his thumb.

"Got it," he said into the phone. He listened and nodded, annoyed. "I know the routine—it was my idea, remember? You've got ten minutes—hold on."

He was interrupted by a sharp rap on the door. It opened, and Trey's father walked in. He stopping short, checked the number on the door, and said, "Who are you … hey, don't I know you?"

"Nah," Ewen said, shaking his head in disgust. "You've got the wrong guy." He turned away and said into the phone in a low voice, "I gotta go—make it quick." He brushed past Trey's father, and was out the door without a parting word.

Trey's father looked at me and said, "Some people never learned basic manners."

I stared back. He couldn't expect a response, which left me confused, as it always did. Should I ignore him and seem rude? Could a ferret *be* rude?

He glanced around and called for Trey, and then looked at me again. "Where is he?"

I wanted to shrug my little shoulders, dramatically, sarcastically, but the very thought of such an action sent shivers of panic down my back.

He looked around again. "Son-of-a-bitch," he whispered. "I wonder if that guy was—?"

"Dad?"

Trey had come through the door.

"Where've you been?" the father said.

Trey waved his hand vaguely. "Some jerk dragged me away to show me a poster he'd pinned to the bulletin board. He's running for city council—pretended to want my opinion."

"Politicians are salesmen in love with their product."

"Uh, there was a man here. Is he in the bathroom?"

"He left. I swear I know him. Seemed like he was in a real hurry—"

"He *left?*"

"Yeah. What did he want?"

"It's, uh, complicated," Trey said, flummoxed. He seemed relieved when he saw the manila envelope on the table. He picked it up and peeked inside.

"Try me," his father said.

Trey looked at him and frowned. "Dad, I can't tell you. I'm sorry."

"What do you mean you can't tell me? What's the big secret?" He furrowed his brow. "I know I've seen that guy before." His eyes brightened. "I remember. It was months ago. One of the tenants over at Vista Grande called me in from next door where I was putting in a faucet. She must be ninety, and half senile. A guy—*that* guy—was trying to sell her some kind of insurance, and she wanted me to tell her what to do. She thought I was her son. As soon as I asked to look at the paperwork, he took off—just like now!"

"Dad, you just thought it was the same man. It can't be. Remember when you were so positive that Jennifer Garner in *Juno* was Julia Roberts, you bet me ten dollars?"

"Yeah, yeah. That was different. Hey, did I ever pay you?"

"No, Dad. It's okay. Admitting you were wrong was payment enough."

Suddenly, it hit me. I didn't understand what Ewen had been doing to Trey's computer, but he obviously didn't want Trey to know. Something smelled of day-old fish, as someone said. Maybe Trey would understand if he looked at his laptop, but he had pulled the papers out of the envelope and was reading.

I liked Trey. I thought he'd get along nicely with Joanne. If only he'd look at the laptop.

Then I saw it, the little black stick Ewen had plugged into the laptop. It lay there under a small table next to the apartment door. He must have dropped it when Trey's father came in. If Trey saw it, he might know what the man had done to the laptop.

"Did you want something, Dad?" Trey asked.

"Yeah. Can I borrow a shirt?"

"Again?"

"If it's too much to ask for the man who toiled for twenty years so that his son could—"

"Cut it out. Of course you can borrow a shirt. Another date? Anybody I know?"

"Same as the last one."

"A second date? That's a first. You may have to invest in your own shirt—two, even."

"Maybe. Let's see if she can balance her checkbook first."

"Mom couldn't."

"Exactly."

"Well, step into my salon," Trey said as he slowly opened the bedroom door and stuck his foot through to hold back the frantic dog.

I waited until Trey's father went through and closed the door. I was sure now that Ewen had been up to something nefarious. Based on how long Joanne spent picking out clothes for her dates, I guessed that it would be many minutes before the two men came out. The latch on the portable kennel cage was the same as Joanne's—an easy mechanism to undo once I brought all my meager ferret muscle to bear. The harder part would actually be latching it again when I returned.

Once out, I paused on the table top. Trey's muffled voice came through the closed door, rising and falling in tone, cut off by the monotone of his father. I jumped down, a long way for a ferret, and rolled on the soft carpet. Shaking my head to clear it, I found the black stick and nosed it. This was quite odd. Why would Ewen stick a little flashlight into Trey's laptop? He hadn't, I decided. This wasn't the black stick. He must have slipped that into his pocket.

Just then, the bedroom door swung open, and Trump blasted through, ahead of a protesting curse from Trey's father. I froze. Maybe he wouldn't notice me. The white face scanned the room, knowing I must be here somewhere. The curly fur suggested comical impotence, but the little teeth could do real damage to a like-sized creature. Like me.

It was inevitable. The fierce eyes found me, and the little devil launched into a frenzied storm of alarmed barking, as though he'd caught me ready to pounce from my hiding place. Alternating between squealing barks and threatening growls, he crouched low, then jumped forward, causing me to lean away, which he must have interpreted as a counter attack, sending him back with a yelp, only to turn around and renew the battle cry with a higher pitch and vigor.

I heard Trey's phone tweedling as he scooped up Trump, kicking and squirming, swearing that if Trey would just let him down, he'd make quick work of this dangerous intruder.

"Yeah, Desmond?" Trey said over incessant barking. "*What?*" he croaked incredulously as he handed the fluid dog to his father. "That can't be!" he yelled, going to his laptop. He lay the phone on the table and tapped away, jabbing each key forcefully, as though playing timbales. He stared at the screen and shook his head in disbelief. He slammed the lid closed and picked up the phone. "He left just minutes ago—yeah. Yeah. But—yeah. Yeah! Shit!" Trey poked at the phone and laid it back on the table. He stood staring into nothing.

"Son," his father said above the barking. He wrapped his big hand around the dog's snout. "Son, what happened?"

Trey turned to look at him, his gaze seeming to glide through his father and off to some fearful place in the distance. "He got into my bank account."

His father tightened his hand over the squirming dog. "Ah, geez. He got your bonus, son." He shook his head. "I told you it was a mistake to post it—"

"It's not the money," Trey said, suddenly present, suddenly angry.

"Not the money? What, then? The principle? I'd trade principle for cash any day—"

"No!" Trey said, waving his hand as though physically shoving the whole subject aside. "It's, it's …" He stopped, again staring at nothing. He sat heavily in a chair and buried his face in his hands. "It was all a lie," came muffled words. "None of it true."

Slowly at first, like a train building steam, his shoulders rose and fell. Short sniffles became sobs.

Holding the dog with one hand, his father put his other one on his son's shoulder. "Son, what's wrong?"

Trey suddenly sat up straight and pounded both fists on the table. He turned a wet face to his father. "I was going to live forever."

His father blinked.

Trey stood up, wiping his sleeve across his eyes. "It was stupid. *I* was stupid."

"Son, I don't understand—"

"It doesn't matter, Dad. I'd rather not talk about it. It's embarrassing." He took a deep breath and looked at the open door of the cage, then found me crouched under the small table. "How'd he get out?"

His father shrugged. "You must not have latched the door."

"No. I did. I'm sure. I've done it a million times." He turned quizzical eyes back to me, and I started to shiver. "He let himself out," he said, amazed.

The shivering made my vision shake.

"Nah," his father said.

"Yes! He did!" He peered at me. "That is one damn intelligent ferret."

Just then, Trump heaved a mighty jerk and exploded from the father's grip. He landed on the carpet running, and came straight for me. I don't know what happened next. I went catatonic.

∞

So, here I sit on Trey's dresser in Trump's carry cage. Trey has secured the door with twists of wire. I could undo this, of course, but I'd go catatonic again when he found out.

Living with Trey won't be so bad. I'll miss Joanne desperately. My short time with her will forever be the golden era, the heaven I took for granted. It could be worse. I could be eating rats in the alley.

I will have to deal with Trump, though. He's a small dog. One semi-sweet chocolate bar should do it.

Chapter 4

Hello old familiar dresser. Blessed dresser. I shall be forever indebted to Trey, my knight in shining armor—although I suspect that a Medieval knight would have probably roasted a ferret for dinner before thinking to find its owner. Okay, Trey will forever be my first-responder hero, something more current.

This makes me sound like a human female. I know I'm not the former, and I suspect—let me check … no, I am definitely not the latter either.

We'll leave it that Trey is simply a hero.

Where was I? Yes, I was explaining how I arrived back at this, my original 8:00 PM reporting post. Trey was true to his word, and posted notices about me. Not only did he post them in his building, but the adjacent apartments as well, for which he earns the title Head Supreme Hero, since I had chosen the wrong wing as Joanne's. Before the day was out, I was snuggling against Joanne's face as she tried to get Trey to accept a reward. Instead of a monetary reward, he suggested going for coffee sometime.

If the universe offers compensation for horrible endurances, I am glad I ate the rat.

Luck was on a roll. Joanne—we—are leaving tomorrow to visit her parents. Had Trey not been prompt in advertising my loss, somebody might have tacked a different notice on top of his by the time she returned.

Off to bed in my own luxury cardboard box with the hole cut in the side. I am a little wary about sleeping, however. Last night I had another nightmare. I had let myself out of my cage, intent on helping Trey—how, and for what reason, I don't know—but this time, Trump caught my neck in his jaws, which had suddenly grown huge, and he swallowed me. When I woke, trembling, I wasn't sure at first if perhaps the darkness was that of Trump's stomach. First the nightmare with Duncan, and now this. My little subconscious must be heeding the taboo about revealing my intelligence.

∞

To whom it may concern. To whomever has caused me to come to a dresser at 8:00 PM and think about the day just passed. It seems I spend more time on dressers other than Joanne's. As I lay here in my cage, I can hear conversation downstairs. I wish I could be there, lying in Joanne's lap, but, alas, I am a ferret, and ferrets are often banished to cages.

There's no lack of things to review this evening. Forgive me if I summarize at times, whoever you are. Otherwise it could take the whole night. The day began on a high note—both metaphorical and literal, since Joanne hums tunes from animated movies when she's happy. She was packed, prepped, and perfumed when Trixie arrived to pick us up. Trixie owns a car, a car new enough to get us confidently the sixty or so miles to Joanne's parents.

Trixie has been Joanne's friend since college. Her real name is Carolyne, and, according to Trixie, she got the nickname when she was seven and convinced her younger brother to hold the end of the garden hose, telling him that he had to watch and see if he could grab the wedding ring that their mom had dropped down the sink. Meanwhile, Carolyne ran around the corner and turned on the spigot full, throwing a gush of water into his sputtering face. A few days later, she did it again, assuring him that the first time had been mishandled, but this time they'd get it right. When she ran back around the corner, he was holding the hose away from his dripping face yelling that she had "trixed" him—she was a "trixie trixer."

The name had stuck.

In junior high, she lived up to the moniker, finding clowning around to be a preferred alternative to the constant, seemingly fruitless effort to fit in with the right clothes, gossip, and snarky phrasing. In high school the clowning evolved into subtle sabotage of teacher authority, winning her membership in the too-cool-to-care outcast crowd. By college, she had figured out that she'd been shooting herself in the foot, and buckled down to study. A lifetime of dancing around the boundaries of society, however, had instilled a perspective askew of authority in general. She expected anybody intent on picking up the hose to douse her. Over the course of four college years, maturing into adult rebellion, she gravitated towards the philosophical camp most suspicious of authority.

She was, as Joanne's mother whispered alarmingly, a liberal. I learned all this as Joanne chatted with her mom while they made lunch.

But I'm getting ahead of myself.

Joanne's parents live an hour away in suburbs that settled in for a life of quiet comfort fifty years ago. Over the decades, the track housing blandness melted as trees matured, and owners deposited savings back into their best-life-investment with family room additions and detached garages. Some, like Joseph McCullagh, her parent's neighbor, used extraordinary fortune to reach beyond mere investment supplement to create an island of conspicuous wealth in the sea of no-nonsense development, a little enclave of Hollywood extravagance. He replaced the one-car driveway with a half-circle that swept past a regal entranceway guarded on each side by Pantheon columns, and substituted their common-sense asphalt shingles for Spanish style tiles. An enlarged pool in the back cuddled next to a small guest house. With money collected dollar-by-dollar from a congregation thousands deep and a nation wide, he exposed, by contrast, the ordinary lives of factory supervisors, plumbers, and accountants that surrounded them.

Trixie had never met Joanne's parents, and from the backseat, happily sprawled in my own carry cage, I heard her ask Joanne what she should know. "My folks are the definition of normal," Joanne said. "Dad and Mom married when they were nineteen, and Bobby—"

"Your older brother?"

"Yes. Bobby was born seven months later."

"That's normal?"

"For the time. Unwed mothers weren't all that exceptional in Glendale, but my grandparent's generation still felt faint at the thought of checking off the 'single' box on the hospital admission form when their daughter finally went into labor."

"Your parents wouldn't mind if you decided to be a single mother?"

Joanne didn't answer right away. "Yeah, they'd mind," she finally said. "Fortunately, I don't intend to walk up to that bridge."

"Because suitors are lined up at your door?"

"Ho, ho. I just couldn't do it. I'm not that strong. This guy is about all I can handle."

I lifted my head to see that she had tilted her thumb back towards me.

"So," Trixie said, "your parents are totally old school."

"Hmm. I guess, if old school means conservative. I guess that's the definition of conservative. Resist change."

"That's the old definition—the conservative definition of conservative. The new definition is thick-headed and mean. If you're conservative, you have to broadcast the fact, make sure your tribe can trust you. You start by declaring that immigrants on the southern border are either drug dealers and murderers, or lazy loafers looking to suck on the teat of government largess. Then, you move on, shrugging off the 'hoax' of global warming so that you can convince yourself that environmental regulations are liberal attacks on corporations, although why liberals are out to get corporations in the first place is not explained—"

"Trixie."

"What?"

"Are you going to behave?"

"I always behave."

"Mostly badly."

"You didn't tell me you were dragging me into a den of conservatives."

Joanne looked at her and shook her head. "It takes two to polarize, you know."

"Whose side are you on, anyway?"

She stared out the side window before answering. "I'd like to say that I'm on everybody's side. The reality, though, is that I end up on nobody's side."

"That's awfully bleak."

Joanne sighed. "Simple survival."

"Right. So, you'd like undocumented immigrants who've been living here most their lives, working every day, raising a family, to be hauled away."

"I didn't say that."

"You want the feds to get out of the healthcare business completely. Survival of the fittest. If you can't make enough money to afford insurance, deductibles, and co-pays, well then, your kids should die and remove your deficient genes from the pool."

"Don't be ridiculous."

"Sounds to me like you're a flaming liberal, gal."

"Once you brand yourself as anything—conservative or liberal—you've locked in your positions. From that point on, all your opinions are established, and not by you."

"You believe our tax dollars should fund private charter schools?"

"Trixie, you know I don't. Look, I try to examine every issue on its own. It just so happens that I usually end up siding with what's considered a liberal stance."

"Oh, really? Name one issue where you side with conservatives."

She thought a moment. "I believe that we should balance the budget. The federal debt is way too high."

"Ha! That was a conservative position, like, three decades ago. When was the last time you heard a conservative pundit talk about the debt? Republicans abolished slavery, you know—now look where they stand."

"Fine, fine. Call me a liberal, then, if that will keep you quiet."

"Liberal," Trixie said, looking ahead at the road. She turned to Joanne. "Liberal, liberal, liberal."

"You done now?"

"I think so. Wait. Liberal. Okay, now I'm done."

∞

Joanne's mother must have been watching for us, since she was out the door and waving before Trixie and Joanne unbuckled their seatbelts. She is a handsome woman, by ferret sensibilities at least, and Joanne's father, following along behind, although probably a little too thick around the waist to be considered healthy, seemed congenial enough. Trixie's disdained descriptions had fostered an image of some sort of dour-faced ogre.

When Joanne lifted my cage out from the back, her father frowned, though, and said, "You brought the animal."

"Dad, Chewy is an animal."

"He's not a wild animal."

"A ferret is as much a pet as a dog."

Her father shrugged. "I suppose you'll want to let it out."

"Sometimes. We can't leave him in the cage all day long—"

"Which means we'll have to keep Chewy down in the rec room."

"It won't kill him for an hour or two."

I was just beginning to think that maybe he was a bit of an ogre when he broke out in a grin and held out his arms for a hug. "Chewy won't mind. He considers it worth it to have you home for a while."

My little round ears perked up at that. Was this a fellow sentient animal? It was a fleeting thought, for I realized that if the dog were truly sentient, its owner wouldn't have to worry that it would maul a ferret purely out of canine instinct. This was confirmed when Joanne carried my cage inside past an aging boxer lying on a folded blanket in a corner. His ears twitched when he saw me, and he struggled to his feet and followed along with raspy, insistent barks, sounding the alarm that a foreign creature, probably maleficent, had managed to infiltrate the homeland. After a few feet, he paused, exhausted, and settled back to the floor.

Joanne set me down in a corner as her mother puttered around the kitchen and the rest eased into chairs at the table. Within minutes, she was pouring coffee into mugs while Joanne stared at a mountain of homemade blueberry muffins and strawberry tarts on a plate so large, there was hardly any room to set the mugs down. "Mom, you promised not to go crazy with food."

"I didn't, dear," she replied, dispersing a platoon of chocolate cookies across terraced, sugar-mined slopes. "I was planning on making these anyway."

"What? Dad's entire Masonic lodge is stopping by?"

"Always the dramatist," her mother said, sitting down with her own mug. "Your father likes my desserts."

"You made all this for Dad?" Joanne challenged. "He's lucky we showed up. Dad, are you determined to become obese in your retirement?"

"Leave me out of it," he said, pulling off the biggest piece of tart from the pile.

Joanne watched the slab of sweet doughy goo as it sailed for a landing on his plate. "Looks like you're climbing into it," she said. "So, how's retirement going? Two months in Mom's hair all day long, and she hasn't killed you yet."

"Fine," he said, working at the tart with his fork.

"Just fine? I thought you couldn't wait to but down the trowel?"

Her mother and father glanced at each other. "Your father isn't exactly completely retired," her mother said.

Joanne looked at each in turn. "The union lets you work part-time?"

Her father gave a sigh, and her mother watched him, her brow worried. "He isn't working for the union."

"Really? Is that, like, legal?"

Her father pushed the tart away. "I left the union when I retired."

"Dad, I don't understand. Why are you working?"

"It's just temporary."

"That's not an answer."

"It's just to get us over a hump. It's no big deal."

"The transmission went in the car," her mother said quietly, as though this would keep her husband from hearing. "While it was in the garage, the furnace blew up."

"The furnace didn't 'blow up,'" her father said.

"That's what you said."

"I was upset."

"I'll bet you were," Joanne said. "That's why you're working?"

Her father poked at the tart.

"We can't go without heat," her mother explained.

"But, but …" Joanne looked at Trixie who raised her eyebrows and shrugged. "What about savings?"

Her mother re-arranged a couple of cookies on the mound. This was for her husband to address.

"Dad?" Joanne said.

"Social security and the pension covers our costs," he said without looking up.

"Apparently not. You don't *have* any savings?"

"Of course we do."

"But, like, you don't want to use it? I don't understand—"

"It's not enough," her mother said sharply, glancing at her husband.

"Middle America living on the razor's edge," Trixie said. "The median American household savings is less than five thousand dollars, and forty percent of adults wouldn't be able to cover a four-hundred-dollar emergency—"

Joanne held up her hand to be quiet.

"I was just trying to help," Trixie said. "Their situation is not unusual—"

Joanne pumped her hand, putting the brakes on Trixie's mouth. "Dad, do you need money? I don't have a lot of savings, but—"

"The bills are paid. Enough, already. Trixie, what do you do?"

"Annoy my friends, mostly. Otherwise, I'm a barista."

"A barista. That's like a bartender for coffee?"

"I'm supposed to say that I'm an *artiste* of caffeinated delights, but I sling mojo—"

"Dad," Joanne said, interrupting, "did you take a loan on the house?"

"No! Enough, now."

"You had to borrow from *somebody*—"

"He borrowed it from Joseph," her mother said.

"Joseph McCullagh? The holy roller?"

"Joanne," her mother chastised, "Joseph is helping us out. Your father's working off the loan."

"Dad's working for *him*? You should have called me—"

"You don't have that kind of money," her father said, "and you know it. Now, that's enough. I mean it."

They all poked at their desserts in silence. "Hey," Trixie finally said, "you're actually helping this Joseph guy out as well. This little act of charity will get him one small step closer to heaven. Although, I guess if it was truly charity, he'd just give you the money—"

She shut up when Joanne's father glared at her.

They nibbled half-heartedly at the desserts. "Trixie," Joanne's father said, attempting to break the ice-jam, "you're able to live in the city on your coffee shop pay?"

"Barely, and not without help," she said. "I have a roommate."

"Uh, but not with Joanne, right? You live alone, don't you, honey?"

"Not at all," Joanne said. She pointed at me. "Rascal is all the company I can handle. He's tons of trouble sometimes, but he's my buddy. I wouldn't give him up for the world."

"In fact, he saved her a few days ago," Trixie said, looking at Joanne with a little smirk.

Joanne's Mom looked sharply at Joanne, who was giving Trixie an equally sharp look—this was clearly a subject she didn't want brought up. "What happened?" her mother said.

Joanne bit off a large piece of cookie and chewed forcefully.

"Rascal fought off some unwelcome company," Trixie said. "He rectified, shall we say, a bad choice."

Joanne's mother looked searchingly at her daughter. "Honey, what happened?"

"Ah, it's no big deal. Trixie's just teasing."

"But, what happened?"

"Oh, this guy I was dating got a little aggressive—"

"You didn't mention that you were dating somebody."

"It wasn't serious—"

Trixie cleared her throat loudly.

"It wasn't *going* anywhere," Joanne said. "Like I said, no big deal."

"How did your ferret fight off a man?" her mother asked. "He *bit* him?"

Joanne sighed. "Rascal knocked a vase off a shelf."

Her mother wrinkled her brow, perplexed. "He bruised the man's foot?"

Joanne took a deep breath, closed her eyes a moment, and said, "This guy pushed me down on my bed, and—"

"Honey! He was trying to *rape* you?"

"I wouldn't go that far—"

"I think *he* was trying to go that far," Trixie said.

"Oh, honey!" Joanne's mother exclaimed, placing her fingertips to her mouth. "I *knew* you shouldn't have moved to the city. Howard, tell her!"

Her father had been watching the interplay darkly. He shook his head and lifted a chunk of strawberry tart to his mouth. "Like she's going to listen to me? When was the last time she listened to anything I had to say?"

"Howard …!" her mother pleaded.

"Fine," he said, placing his fork down loudly. "Joanne, I want you to move back home."

Joanne glared at him.

"So, will you?" he demanded.

"Of course not, Daddy. You know that."

Her father lifted both hands to the side, palms up, and gave his wife an exaggerated *are you satisfied?* scowl.

Joanne's mother watched her husband and daughter as they returned distractedly to their plates.

"Well, Trixie," her mother finally said, "I only hope you and your roommate watch out for each other."

Trixie grinned. "The roommate was the problem … although, in my case, the activity was consensual. Actually, I'm usually the one getting the ball rolling, if you know what I mean—"

It was Joanne's turn to clear her throat, even louder than Trixie had.

"What?" Trixie said.

I wasn't sure if she was genuinely surprised.

Joanne sighed again. "Trixie's roommate is actually her boyfriend."

"I see," her mother said, a little dazed. "Trixie … you said that he was a … problem, though?"

"Not him per se. Well, yeah, I guess his sperm is technically 'him'—"

"That's it!" Joanne exclaimed. She slapped her hands on the table, and stood up. Her face was bright red. "Christ almighty," she said. "Trixie got pregnant, and had an abortion. There, I hope everybody's satisfied." She looked like she was going to add to that, but instead, she pushed back her chair. "I'm going to unpack."

She grabbed her bag in one hand, lifted my cage with the other, sending me staggering from one side to the other, and stomped out of the room and up the stairs. Her father shouted to her back, "Watch your mouth, young lady!"

∞

"You promised," Joanne said.

"Not true," Trixie replied, hands behind her head, eyes closed, her face turned up to the sun as they lounged in the backyard. "You asked if I was going to behave, and I replied that I always behave. It's one of those subjective concepts, driven by the perspective of the individual."

I lay curled in Joanne's lap, the ferret brain insistent we go exploring, but I glued us in place, determined to see how things would turn out.

"Bullshit," Joanne said. "Can you honestly tell me that you didn't know my parents would be bothered that you had an abortion?"

"So, you're telling me that 'behaving' is hiding from the truth?"

"Nobody was hiding, girl. You pulled it unsolicited out of your ass."

Trixie opened her eyes and looked at her friend. "Your language deteriorates the shorter the distance between you and your conservative parents, sort of an inverse relationship. Have you thought about the psychological underpinnings of this?"

"It's not my parents who elicit the bad language."

"I understand," Trixie said. She waited a precise comedian's pause. "Ferrets can indeed be exasperating."

Joanne uttered another, even cruder, word.

"Well, well," came a man's voice from behind their lounge chairs. They turned to find a dapper, handsome gentleman with a close-trimmed gray beard standing there, arms akimbo. "Can it be little Joanne?"

Holding me in both arms, she rolled off the chair and stood up. "Hello, Joseph," she said, moving me to the crook of one elbow so that she could shake his extended hand.

He glanced at Trixie, who had swiveled around, but remained seated. "I stopped to talk to your father," he said. "He told me you'd come to visit with a friend. What he didn't tell me was how attractive she is," he added, moving his gaze to Trixie.

"Really?" Trixie said. "You think so? Huh. Maybe I should try making a little money on the side—"

"Behave," Joanne said.

Joseph watched them, smiling, as though this was a little show created just for him.

Joanne's brow contracted. "Joseph, I want to thank you for helping my father—you know, with the loan."

He bowed his head a little, a modest acceptance of deserved thanks. "Of course, there are two hands reaching out to help," he said.

"Two hands?"

"The loan, and the means to work it off," Trixie said, watching him with one raised eyebrow.

He nodded. "A complete package. Your father's putting in a stone wall along the back. Excellent work. A real craftsman."

"Hourly, or fixed cost?" Trixie asked.

He looked at her, as though waiting for her to reveal something about herself, as though there wasn't a question hanging unanswered. "I believe Joanne's father is satisfied with the arrangement," he finally said.

"So, fixed cost, then. Did her father have any say in the details——?"

"Trixie! Sorry, Joseph. My friend likes to ruffle feathers."

He continued to look at Trixie, tilting his head a little, as though faced with an intriguing puzzle. "No problem. I understand completely her concern. There are certainly many people—un-Christian people—who will take advantage if they can. Trixie just needs to get to know me, like you do, Joanne." He smiled, originating an idea for yet another helping hand. "In fact, why don't the four of you—five, if you'd like to bring the pet ferret—come for tea this afternoon? I'll arrange a time with your parents."

Without waiting for a reply, he gave a little bow and walked away.

Trixie watched him until he turned the corner around the house. "Well," she said turning to Joanne, "the claim is that you know him. Is he really as fake as he seems?"

Joanne was staring towards the corner where he'd disappeared. She broke her gaze and turned to Trixie. "I haven't seen him since I moved away."

"Well? Fake? Or, genuinely slimy?"

"Why would somebody fake being slimy?"

"Good point. He must be genuine."

∞

Joanne didn't want to leave me with Chewy, no matter how infirm the aged dog, so I was back in my cage, legs spread wide for footing as she followed her parents and Trixie down the driveway, along the sidewalk, and around the Cinderella drive into the McCullagh fairyland. It was difficult to see that the original house was the same as the others up and down the street. Dormers with intricate façade eaves sprouted from the sloping roof. Additional rooms had been added, wrapping around the side and back, each hosting high expansive windows, presumably to let light into the buried original rooms within. Stepping through the double-wide doors, Joanne's feet clicked along on hardwood floors, past a statue of a naked man posed as if caught in the throes of dramatic overload, and another of a slim girl in a loose, flowing dress, her angelic face turned downward, as if bashfully accepting a compliment. We walked by a spiral staircase, leading to a landing overlooking the small, open atrium, upon which one might imagine a debutante appearing in brightly colored lace to the appreciative welcome of the gentile crowd below.

Mrs. McCullagh led us to a light and airy room overlooking the pool and guest house, to a round table too small for six people, so that Joanne and Trixie had to sit slightly apart, social satellites, balancing their cups of tea on their knees. A stout Hispanic housekeeper, who they called Maria, served small plates of cookies, which Joanne and Trixie balanced on their other knee. I, as usual, was set in the corner, where I was quickly forgotten, which suited my imprinted instincts just fine.

The conversation ambled along around personal trivia and humorously presented foibles of others not present, following a meandering path as each in turn took up the conversation stick and headed off in a different direction. Despite my ingrained interest in all-things-human, my attention began to wander, and I soon found myself tussling with the nap taboo.

I came to when voices rose in volume and spirit. "Every country has a right to protect its borders," Joanne's father said, the loudest of the debate.

"Protect from what?" Trixie said. "Poor migrant agricultural workers? Destitute mothers and children?"

"We can't have open borders," Joseph said, the mildest voice of the three.

"Nobody's talking about that," Trixie said. "Look, the undocumented workers—"

"Illegals, you mean," Joanne's father corrected.

"The *undocumented* workers went through hell to get here," Trixie pressed on. "Here are people willing to put up with hardships most Americans can't even imagine, let alone shoulder. These are exactly the sort of people we should be welcoming."

Joanne sat, her forehead leaning into both palms. Her mother and Mrs. McCullagh seemed in shock.

"So, you do want open borders," Joseph said mildly.

"No, Joseph," she said emphatically. "Exactly the opposite. Look, they're not taking jobs from US citizens, the facts show it—"

"Liberal elite facts," Joanne's father spat.

"Will you stop cutting me off? They're not taking jobs from Americans. In fact, the economy depends on them. We have a border that's just difficult enough to filter through the hardiest, the most industrious. We'd be stupid to stop this economic source! It's simple logic. It's a perfect balance and you conservatives want to wreck it for the sake of some misguided tribal rallying cry."

"The law is the law!" Joanne's father exclaimed, shouting now. "Most of them come to suck on government handouts. And there's the drugs and the gangs—!"

"No, no! That's bullshit. Almost all the drugs come through ports of entry, and besides, the Central American gangs were actually initiated by those already in Los Angeles, and then we forced the newly indoctrinated gang refugees back to the countries where we supported the anti-communist wars with propped-up dictators in the first place. We *created* the MS-13 gang!"

"No," Joanne's father shouted, almost on his feet now. "*That's* liberal bullshit!"

"No, I'm sorry. That's the facts."

"Facts! Facts! It's all liberal propaganda!"

"If we can't agree on the facts, then there's no debate! It's just shouted arguing! Which, right now, it is!"

"There's facts, and there's facts," Joseph said, still mild, seeming to enjoy his role as the calm, rational one.

Trixie and Joanne's father looked at him. Calm delivery fosters deference.

"The facts you're talking about," he said, gesturing at Trixie, "come from university studies—many funded by tax dollars—and we all know that universities are bastions of liberal thought—"

"That's more conservative bullshit—!" she started, but stopped when he held up his hand and stared her down.

"No cutting off, remember?" he said. "As I was saying, although the media tends to ignore them, there are other institutions of learned study that compile careful figures—"

"Like the Heritage Foundation?" Trixie said with a tone suggesting that the organization was an after-school TV show.

Joseph sat back and crossed his arms on his chest.

"I cut you off again," Trixie said. "That wasn't cool."

Joseph just stared at her.

"Sorry," she said.

Still he stared.

"I said I was *sorry*."

He raised one eyebrow.

"Fuck you!" she exclaimed.

Time and space froze. I noticed that Maria, the housemaid, was standing in the doorway, eyes wide, a teapot gripped in her hand. She could have been placed among the statues in the atrium.

Trixie saw her as well, and she pointed at the stunned middle-aged woman. "I'll bet she's undocumented—excuse me, illegal! What a fucking hypocrite!"

Once the word was let loose, it scampered about, barking at anything it thought the least bit disagreeable.

Mrs. McCullagh recovered enough to shoe Maria away with a dismissive flip of her hand.

Joseph's eyes narrowed. "You don't know what you're talking about. You had better watch your mouth, young lady."

"I'm not your daughter. You can't send me to my room."

He lowered his head, as though about to charge. "I think you had better leave."

Joanne released her forehead, stood up, walked over and picked up my cage, and motioned to Trixie. "Come on, let's go," she said, and my world rocked like a ship floundering in a storm sea, rushing past the reefs of statues and spiral stairs.

∞

"I don't want to hear it," Joanne said, lying on her back on the bed.

"Why not?" Trixie asked. She was sprawled on the floor with her head at the bedroom door, which she'd opened a crack.

"First, it's a private conversation, and second, it's painful. It's bad enough that everybody's in shock from your social grenades. I don't need to also hear how my parents think I'm a total loser."

We'd been holed up in Joanne's old bedroom for the last hour, ever since being ejected from afternoon tea. At least now I was free to explore. The ferret brain wanted to tunnel under the covers, but I pulled him away—I didn't want to miss any human activity.

"I was the one lobbing the grenades," Trixie said, "you just sat there. Besides, your parents love you, Joanne. Unconditionally, remember?"

"Yeah, yeah. I think they can love and hate me all at the same time—"

"Shh! I think Joseph's here—yeah, it's him."

Joanne sat up, almost knocking me off the bed. "What's he saying—?"

"Shh!"

I heard talking downstairs, but couldn't make out the words. I was about to jump down from the bed and get closer, but that would have been a little to un-ferret-like.

"Uh, oh," Trixie said.

"What're they saying—?"

"Shh!" Trixie listened and then turned her head to look at Joanne. Her face said the news was not good. "Maria has left."

"Left ... gone for the day?"

"Disappeared. Gone for good. My grenade was a little too accurate."

Joanne hopped down and came to the door on hands and knees. "Oh God. What have we done?"

"All you did was bring along the grenade launcher. Joseph is really mad. He wants compensation."

"That's crazy!" Joanne hissed. "He's demanding compensation because he hired an undocumented worker?"

"Conservative hypocrisy knows no logic. He wants an extra eighty hours from your father. He wants him to put in a fountain when the wall is complete."

"The bastard!"

"I was thinking of another description. Want to hear it?"

Joanne stood up and reached for the doorknob, but Trixie caught her wrist. "What do you think you're going to do?"

"I ... first I'm going to call him that name you're thinking, and then I'm going to tell him that I'll call the police if he doesn't back off my Dad."

"Think about it, girl. Calling him names will only work in his favor in front of your parents. As far as the police, Maria's gone, remember? How are you going to prove that she's undocumented?"

Joanne twisted her wrist free and turned around, staring out the window. "What was the name you were thinking?"

"It involves fellatio. It succinctly identifies the 'giver.'"

"I'll keep it in reserve."

∞

Joanne's father had planned on taking the whole day off from wall-building to visit with his guests, but had changed his mind when he found that retirement was now delayed by another eighty hours. Joanne said that he probably just wanted to get out of the house before somebody—like her—got hurt. Joseph had quickly nixed the idea, insisting that he "put family first—it's what Christ would want." After Joseph left, Joanne's mother had shouted up the stairs that they were going out to pick up some groceries for dinner, to which Joanne snorted. "Right. Mom has the menu and all the ingredients ready days before I arrive."

"You know that for a fact?" Trixie asked.

"Do you *have* a mother?" Joanne replied.

So, after peeking to make sure her parents were gone, Joanne led the way out back to the lounge chairs. "What if they come home and catch us out here?" Trixie said, after they settled in.

"My Dad's not dangerous, not physically. I don't remember him ever laying a hand on me or my brother. He makes up for it with stormy silences."

"Uh, isn't that a contradiction?"

"Ever see the towering black clouds of a summer thunder storm just before the first lightning strike? The world is completely calm, but it's a calm pregnant with menace."

"Pregnant with menace, eh? You been reading romance novels again? So, what's with fellatio-giver?"

"Joseph? What do you mean?"

"How did he manage to create his own little Versailles in the middle of Americana suburbs. How'd he get hold of an Anthony Caro, for God's sake?"

"A who-what?"

"Anthony Caro. He was a British sculptor. That was his piece hanging from the ceiling."

"The metal thingy? I thought it was leftover junk from some renovation. How do you know it was Caro?"

"Joseph had a plaque hanging next to it. The font must be, like, two hundred. He wants to make sure everybody knows it's not leftover renovation junk."

"Have you ever heard of the Christ Redemption Disciples Church?"

"Joanne, my dear friend, do I *seem* to you like somebody who would know this?"

"Right. Joseph's church is huge. He started out with a dozen members who met in his living room. When I was a little girl, I thought they were yelling at each other. I wondered what they were all angry about. He built it up, renting and then buying an old town hall, and moving up from there. He left the Baptists behind, since they're suspicious of any organization larger than what can fit in a firehall. His church now rivals Albert Hall in London. Every Sunday over two thousand worshipers crowd in to shout responses to his joyous message of redemption and ever-lasting life. Tens of thousands more tune in on TV."

"Figures. Kind of a long name, though, don't you think?"

"It used to be just Christ Redemption Church, but another mega-church threatened to sue, claiming they thought of it first."

"I guess he doesn't want to be too blatant about getting rich from people's naivete—"

"That's your opinion."

"Of course it is, even though it's true. So, he remains in the same house he started from. Ever so humble—"

Joanne had put her finger against her lips. "Did you hear that?" she whispered.

Trixie tilted her head, listening. "No," she whispered.

I heard it. A girl's giggle, a little nervous.

Joanne looked at her friend expectantly.

Trixie nodded. She stood carefully up, and walked softly to the thick hedge bordering the McCullagh's property. Walking along, moving her head up and down, she tried to look through, but the intertwined branches formed an impenetrable barrier.

This gave me an idea. I jumped off of Joanne's lap, and made straight for the back corner. I found this earlier while exploring. Her father had begun his indentured service there by removing a small cypress in order to start Joseph's wall. This left a small gap in the hedge, not obvious unless you were right there. Joanne followed, hissing for me to come back. I found the gap even larger than I had remembered, and waited for her to catch up. Without even glancing at it, she reached down and scooped me up. "Behave, Rascal!" she whispered, and started back.

Although there are distinct advantages in having a body that can slide through holes barely large enough for a person's fist, it can also be extremely frustrating sometimes being helpless to the domination—no matter how loving—of your best friend. I'm not some small-brained little animal—actually, I am, but unless I was completely fooling myself, I was sure I had cognitive abilities above par. One full-body squirm freed me, and I raced back to the corner. This time, I stood up on my hind legs and pointedly peered through the gap. Joanne would have had to be blind not to get it, which, of course, she isn't. "Huh," she whispered, her head next to mine. She hissed to get Trixie's attention and waved for her to come. "Well," she whispered to me, "aren't you the smart little guy."

I froze. What had I done? I collapsed, and curled into a ball. Joanne didn't notice as Trixie had arrived, and she pointed through the gap.

"Whoo-hoo," Trixie crooned softly. "What have we here? Who's the floozy?"

"Hmm," Joanne said. "She's not even old enough to be a floozy—she can't be more than sixteen."

"Definitely not eighteen."

"He told my parents he had to leave to host a youth Bible study, and his wife had gone to her spa session. My guess is that the girl's head is still echoing with Bible verses."

"I don't think Joseph's head is in the Bible—look! He's sliding his hand up the back of her blouse. Geez, what a pervert!" Trixie squeaked. "Oh, boy. Hold on," she said sprinting back to the lounge chairs. She returned with her phone. "Move over," she whispered, edging Joanne aside and pointing the phone through the gap just as Joseph leaned down and gave the girl a tender kiss. He put his arm around her shoulder and led her into the guest house. Once inside, he glanced around, and closed the door.

"Son of a bitch," Joanne said, sitting back. "The guy's a child molester!"

Trixie was looking at her phone. "Got him! The slimy predator."

"What are you going to do with it?"

"I'm going to wait right here."

"Why? It could take a while—if she's lucky, I guess. Shit! What am I saying?"

"Confusing, isn't it?"

"Why wait?"

Trixie held the phone so she could see. "You already showed me the picture—oh! There's a timestamp."

"The amount of time inside might be informative."

"Ah. Otherwise, he might say they just went in to get something."

"Okay. I guess we might as well get comfortable. Hey! What's with you?" she said, stroking my fur.

I uncurled. I was still shivering, but at least I hadn't gone catatonic. I stretched, pretending to have woken from a restful snooze.

"We should be so lucky," Trixie said.

"How?" Joanne asked.

"To be a ferret. What a life."

No, girl, I thought. *Ferrets wish they were people so they could talk to other people.*

At least this one does.

∞

I was nosing around a hole emanating a distinctive smell of toad when I saw Joanne and Trixie jump up from their lookout post and run for the house. I scampered after them, but the back door closed before I could get in. This was highly unusual for Joanne to forget about me, meaning that they had something imperative on their minds.

I took a guess, and shot off around the side of the house … to be met by a closed gate. This was meant to keep things out, not in, since I jumped up onto a broken chair, and from there onto a hanging plant, and over the fence. I made it to the front yard just as Joanne and Trixie emerged to immediately make a show to stare and point down the street in the opposite direction from Joseph, pretending to be looking at something. I think they were caught by surprise. They hadn't expected Joseph to be ushering his underaged dalliance date out the front door so soon.

I noticed that Trixie had one fist planted on her hip, and the other hand was holding her phone along the small of her back … pointed back at Joseph. A red light blinked in the corner. She held it there until the girl's car drove past us and away. Joanne peeked over her shoulder to make sure Joseph had gone inside. "Rascal!" she said, seeing me, "what are you doing out here?"

Same thing as you, I thought. I ran over and let her pick me up.

∞

"Looks good," Joanne said, gazing at Trixie's phone. "An American minister pervert in action. The whole clip is just two and a half minutes long. Short and sweet, or, in this case, short and salacious."

Trixie had snipped and pasted together the video pieces for presentation. Now the question was how to present.

"I say we just march over and shove it in his face," Trixie said.

"I don't know," Joanne said, biting her lower lip. "Maybe we should show it to my Mom and Dad first."

"Okay, and since your Dad is directly indebted, I guess for him, that makes it blackmail."

"Really? You think so? That's crazy! Joseph's the criminal!"

Trixie shrugged. "We could go to the police. That won't help your Dad, though."

"Besides," Joanne said, her brow furrowed, "all we really have is a minister going into a building with a teenager." Her face brightened. "He kissed her."

"That hardly constitutes sex with a minor."

Joanne sighed. "Let's march over."

∞

The marching did not include me. After catching me out front, Joanne decided that I needed a little quiet time, i.e., a prison spell. I could have opened the cage door, of course, but if she happened to catch me before I returned, she'd be convinced of my sentience, and that would mean catatonia for me, maybe permanently.

I lay and listened to her mother downstairs preparing dinner. Voices suddenly bubbled up, Joanne and Trixie, a little too loud, anxious to get past Joanne's mother. "You could help with the salad!" her mother called as feet pounded up the stairs.

From the bedroom doorway, Joanne yelled, "Okay! I'll be down in a minute! I have to ... brush my teeth!"

"Ho, boy," Trixie said, closing the door and standing with her back flat against it, as though preventing anybody from forcing their way through. She yanked her phone from her pocket and poked at it, making sure the incriminating evidence hadn't evaporated.

"Oh, man," Joanne agreed.

This didn't tell me a lot. "*What happened?*" I wanted to shout, but my larynx is practically useless.

"Did you see the spittle at the corner of his mouth?" Trixie said. "I thought he was going to punch us both."

Joanne closed her eyes and nodded, relieved to have it over. "He agreed, though."

"Yeah," Trixie said, abandoning her door-guard position to flop onto the bed. "How do you think he's going to present it to your Dad? Just out of the blue, tell him he decided that he doesn't have to work the extra eighty hours?"

Joanne shrugged. "Sure. He's a minister. He'll explain that Christ told him to do it.

Joanne's face turned worried. "Do you think he'll call the police?"

"He's not that stupid. There's no way he could keep that quiet. What would he tell his wife? Besides, it's his word against ours." She laughed. "You told your mother that you had to urgently brush your teeth."

"What was I going to say? Take a crap?"

"One could imagine scenarios of urgency."

∞

And, so, Joanne's childhood dresser, here I lay, listening to Joanne, and Trixie, and Joanne's parents downstairs. I can't discern individual words, but it sounds as though Joanne's father has maybe forgiven her. This, not even knowing what she and Trixie have done for him.

Goodnight. I think my napping taboo is finally lifting for the day and I can sleep now.

∞

Hello, Joanne's adult dresser. Back home—Joanne's home, my home. Everybody was tired and a bit dazed today, having been awake most of the night. On top of that, I nearly burst my brain. But you, whoever is listening (if there even is somebody listening now) may already know all about this.

Regardless, I will explain, since that is my role now at 8:00 PM.

After the long day tussling with Joseph, I fell into a deep sleep, woken once when Joanne and Trixie came to bed, and then again later from another strange dream—a nightmare, where I crawled up and up a pile of rocks so that I could see through a gap in the hedges, and when I finally looked through, Joseph was right there with a bat cocked. He swung it, and I woke shivering. It took a while to fall back to sleep, and when I woke a third time, the room was dark and silent. No dream this time, so I wondered what had woken me.

And then I smelled Joseph.

At first I thought it might just be remnants of his scent on Joanne or Trixie's cloths, but I would have detected it earlier, and it was too strong, too present.

I heard rustling. Beyond the bottom of the bed.

I didn't know what he was up to, but whatever his intentions, I didn't want to be trapped inside the cage. I reached up to unlatch the door, and a wave of fear set me trembling, not from Joseph, but the ill-defined inhibition to reveal my intelligence. Joanne—and Trixie—could be in real danger, while my fear was ... fabricated. Something, or somebody, wanted to conceal my intelligence, but they couldn't stop me from using it.

I reached out and undid the latch, but my trembling paw shook the door.

The rustling abruptly stopped. My cage sat on the dresser, level with Joanne and Trixie's heads, where they both lay asleep. Joseph stood up, just a dark mass, but his scent was unmistakable. He lay something down on the chair—Joanne's handbag—and came quietly around the opposite side of the bed. He paused and leaned over, looking at Joanne, while, despite my shaking, I stepped out of the cage as quietly as I could. Joseph turned and came back around the bottom of the bed to my side. He stood right next to me, peering at Trixie.

And then I saw it, lit by the gentle glow of the alarm clock. Trixie's phone lay on the night stand next to her. Just the corner showed, the rest covered by a tissue. This, of course, was what he was after, the damning video.

He must have seen it at the same time, and reached for it. In the fraction of a second that I had to decide, I saw no other course. Slamming aside the inhibiting fear, I launched myself into the air, coming down on Joseph's outreached hand. I was not able to harm a human, or, at least, this was supposed to be the case. I might as well have been digging my own eyes from their sockets, but my determination sprang from an anger deeper than the inhibition, anger at being manipulated, held by chains in my own mind. One paw caught is arm, and the other, the top of his hand. I clenched, driving my nails into his flesh, and heard a very satisfying scream as my thoughts faded, and I fell, senseless, to the floor.

When I came to, I was met by a lit room and much arguing. Somebody—probably Joanne—had picked me up, and set me on the dresser. Joseph stood back near the closet with his hands out, as though demonstrating that he had no weapons. "I still don't understand what you're doing here," Joanne's father said, his hair tousled into a little tent. Her mother stood in the doorway, the tips of her fingers planted flat against her mouth.

Joseph opened his mouth, and then closed it without saying anything. He looked at Joanne, who stood, hands on indignant hips next to the bed. Trixie was sitting up in the bed, leaning her back against the wall, looking at Joseph while idly flipping her phone from one hand to the other, a communication nobody else noticed.

"Well?" Joanne's father demanded, "what gives?"

The sound of a car stopped outside, accompanied by red light flashing in the trees outside the bedroom window.

"Did he touch either of you girls?" Joanne's father asked without taking his eyes off Joseph.

"No," Trixie said. "He's not interested in *us*."

"Dammit, Joseph," Joanne's father said as the doorbell sounded and her mother ran to get it, "what do you have to say for yourself?"

"I ... I was confused," Joseph finally said.

"I'll say you were. How in hell did you end up in the bedroom?"

"Well, I used the key you gave me years ago, when we exchanged—"

"I figured that. I mean why did you come in here?"

Joseph looked stricken. Still holding his hands out as though ready for a quick draw grab at a holstered six-shooter, he could have been facing a firing squad. He shook his head, no answer available.

Two policemen, a man and a woman, stepped into the room, and Joanne's father moved to the side. "What's going on?" the woman asked, not exactly friendly.

"This is our neighbor," Joanne's father said. "My daughter and her friend woke to find him in their room."

The policewoman raised one eyebrow. "Is this true?" she said to Joseph.

He looked at her, eyes wide. He shook his head, not obvious whether denying, or flummoxed.

"Sir," she said to Joseph, taking his elbow, "would you please step outside?"

He nodded, dazed, and let her lead him away. Just before he stepped through the doorway, Trixie called out, "We're done with the wall, right?"

Joseph stopped and looked back. A glimmer of hope relaxed one layer of terror. He gave a quick nod, and the policewoman urged him on.

"What was all that about?" Joanne's father asked when the male cop left after getting statements from everybody, except me.

"You may want to drop any charges," Trixie said.

"Why? He's lost his mind. He could be dangerous!"

Joanne and Trixie looked at each other. "I didn't think about that," Trixie said.

Joanne took the phone from Trixie and held it up. "Looks like you have a tough decision to make, Dad."

∞

It's a relief to be home again on my own dresser (I now think of it as my own), but as tired as I am, I am resisting, battling, actually, going to sleep. I don't want to even imagine what nightmare will be waiting this time.

By the way, in the end, Joanne's father decided to finish the wall and work off his debt so that Joseph would never again molest underage girls … at least until his prison time is done.

Chapter 5

Hello dresser. I did finally fall asleep last night, and my struggle was vindicated when I dreamt that Joanne was sitting in a chair with her back to me, and somebody—actually I saw just the arm holding a club—was sneaking up from behind. I knew that I was not supposed to interfere, but I decided to anyway. I jumped and caught the hand, and there was a pause. This was the real decision point. My decision had already been made, though, when I had attacked Joseph. I dug my claws into flesh, and, instantly, I was thrown aside. I watched as the club slammed Joanne's head, and she fell off the chair. The next instant, the club came down on me, and I awoke.

This dream repeated each time I fell back asleep.

And, so, dresser, I have very little to report today. I was so groggy, I spent most the time lying, staring, terrified of falling asleep.

I don't know what I will do in the next hours.

∞

Well, dresser, my anxiety was unfounded. Last night I slept soundly, and woke refreshed.

The message is clear.

But from whom? What puppet masters hold my strings, jerking them when I don't submit to their will, and pulling them to drag me here each evening? Joanne sometimes watches an old science fiction TV show, where many scenes are introduced with a voice-over, the lead actor saying, "Captain's log, stardate ..." In the episodes, he's in his space ship, far from Earth. Perhaps for me the roles are reversed, perhaps the listeners are far from Earth. In that case, my nightly recaps would be an Earth log.

Joanne's mother called. She asked when Joanne would come again to visit. She told Joanne that she probably shouldn't be telling her this, but her father wishes he could spend more time with her. Joanne told her mother that right now she's very busy with work, but maybe in a month or so.

After she hung up, Joanne stared at the crossword puzzle in front of her while tapping her pencil on the table. She got up, grabbed her cap, and went out the door, calling over her shoulder, "Back in a little while, Rascal."

This still confuses me. I don't really think that she knows I understand, and why, then, does she do it? Also, she told her mother that she's very busy with work, and I know that she's just going for a walk.

Maybe the work is all done in her head.

∞

Another peaceful night, dresser.

I'll take the reward, no matter how deserved or acknowledged.

Trixie's apartment building is being fumigated for termites. She's going to stay here with Joanne for a few days. Her boyfriend is going to stay with his parents. Joanne told her that she's welcome anytime, but she's curious why she doesn't stay with his parents. "They have three TVs that are turned on when the first person gets up in the morning," Trixie said, "and are turned off when the last person goes to bed."

I know, however, that Trixie has said that his parents think she's a bad influence on him. I wonder if they turn on the TVs only when she comes.

Joanne's mother called again to tell her about a story in their local paper covering Joanne's great aunt, who died a month ago—more or less a memorial celebration of her life, since she was a local artist celebrity. Her work has been shown in New York galleries, and she even once painted President Nixon, although hers was not chosen as the formal version for the National Portrait Gallery. A reporter had previously interviewed Joanne's mother, and when asked about inheritances, she didn't want to reveal too much, so when it came to what her aunt had left to Joanne, she had said, "Oh, let's just say an eight, followed by a few zeroes." In the story, that came out as eight million dollars. When Joanne asked why she hadn't called the paper to correct the mistake, her mother said, "That would have cheapened the memory of your aunt, don't you think?"

When Trixie heard the story during a phone call, she told Joanne, "Your aunt left you eight thousand dollars? What are you still doing in this dinky apartment?"

Joanne held the phone away and gave it a funny look, even though I don't think Trixie could see that. "Have you ever heard of living *under* your means?" she said, putting the phone back to her ear. "The eight thousand would be gone in a year, and I'd be stuck with an apartment I couldn't afford."

"No, no. An expensive apartment would snag you a rich boyfriend."

"What happened to your principle of staunch female independence?"

"Everything has a price," Trixie replied.

∞

Trixie arrived today with six bags. She'll be sleeping on the sofa, and her possessions are spread around it like a coral atoll.

She told Joanne that on the way over, she ran into the family doctor from her childhood. She said that he proves her point that doctors obviously count on their exclusive club—the American Medical Association—to limit membership in their profession in order to keep their pay way up there. The result is overworked doctors, and hers shows the effect—he looks way older than the fifteen years since she last saw him.

She showed him the burn on her thigh that she'd gotten when her boyfriend dropped a soldering iron on her. She laughed at her stereotypical behavior. This was another reason, she explained, that doctors are so stressed—people constantly bothering them outside their office about ailments.

In this case, however, maybe because he has such fond memories of her (I think she was joking), he took an interest. He said that it looked infected, and offered to stop by, since he passes Joanne's apartment building on the way to his office. She liked the idea of a doctor that was still willing to make home visits.

My ears swiveled around when she said his name: Doctor Fenster—Doctor Duncan Fenster.

How do I know what a coral atoll is?

∞

Nothing of import to report. Trey stopped by this evening. He said that he just wanted to see how his previous guest was doing, but he barely gave me a glance once Joanne offered him a glass of wine. Trixie cleared a path through the coral reef, and the three sat on the sofa talking. Joanne and Trixie told him about Joseph, and there was an awkward moment of silence when Trey said in a serious tone, "In a way, though, the teenage girls were communing with God." He looked at the other two, confused. "Hey! I was joking!"

Joanne and Trixie took deep breaths. "Trey likes his humor dark and dry," Trixie said. "My kind of guy."

Another silent void filled the room as Trey glanced quickly at Joanne, who was blushing.

"When I say 'my kind of guy,'" Trixie added, "I don't necessarily mean the kind I want to jump."

This brought blushes to both Joanne and Trey.

Trixie looked at them both and shook her head. "What? Are we in high school? Joanne, Trey wants to ask you out. Trey, ask her out."

"Trey," Joanne said, "I'm really sorry. Trixie is maybe my best friend, but she has the manners of a moose—"

"Joanne," Trey said, "would you like to have dinner with me sometime?"

She looked at him uncertainly, took another deep breath. "Yes, Trey, that would be great." She turned to Trixie and stuck out her tongue.

"So, what's with the 'maybe' my best friend?" Trixie said.

"You're on probation," Joanne replied. "And, right now, you're down three points."

"Hey! I got you a date!"

"True. Okay. You're promoted from probation to apprentice best friend—A-B-F."

When Trey finally left, Joanne and Trixie looked at each other and giggled, and then Trixie accused them again of acting like they were still in high school. "If we were in high school," Joanne said, "I probably would have made the mistake of grading him solely on his looks."

Trixie's eyebrows rose. "In a way, you just did grade his looks."

Joanne nodded consent. "I'm not going to pretend that I find him irresistibly attractive. On the other hand, he's not *un*-attractive, and over time, character and a sense of humor will sustain, while looks fade with familiarity."

Trixie was grinning.

"What?" Joanne said. "I know, I'm waxing philosophical—"

"That's not what I'm laughing about. You're already planning your life with the guy."

Joanne gave her a light backhand slap on her shoulder, which made Trixie laugh all the louder.

Wait. What was I thinking? There *was* something of import today. Duncan came to the apartment this morning to look at Trixie's burn. I hid in Joanne's bedroom. Seeing him, hearing him talk, took me back to the alley and memories of the hell that is destitution in a city. He washed his hands, and after a brief inspection, told her that it was indeed infected. He took a small tube from his coat pocket, and rubbed some cream on the burn, saying, "This is an expensive topical antibiotic." He applied a band-aide that Trixie had found. As he was leaving, he said, "I'll stop by tomorrow to check on it." He nodded, as though agreeing to something nobody had voiced. "That would have cost you eighty dollars at the office," he added matter-of-factly.

"Yeah," Trixie said. "I know. And I have a super high deductible."

He nodded, standing in the doorway.

"Uh," Trixie said. "Oh! Maybe I should give you something. After all, not many people get house calls."

Duncan shrugged, and quickly added, "Perhaps. Rules and all."

"Rules?"

He waved it off, the tedium of explaining minutia. "Bureaucracy—it spreads like melanoma. Thirty dollars should do it."

She blinked. "Sure. Hold on," she said as she retrieved the bills from her wallet.

"Okay, then," he said, shoving the money into his pants pocket. He nodded once, and walked quickly away.

I noticed that he didn't wash his hands before leaving.

∞

Joanne and Trey are out tonight, and I had to sneak out of my cage. I hope this is all going somewhere, dresser. And, of course, when I refer to you, dresser, it's understood (I hope it's understood) that I am referring to whomever is listening right now. Dresser, you are not a simile, nor are you an analogy. You are, my friend, a metaphor.

Did you hear that, listeners?

Trixie put me in the cage after I made her spill tea down her front, and she bumped the burn on her thigh which caused her to curse. I was pretending to be cuddly, but actually trying to get a look at what she was reading on her phone. She didn't latch the door properly, so I was able to escape quietly as she watched TV.

When Trey came by to pick up Joanne, the three sat and talked awhile over wine. Trey recounted his misadventure with Ewen. He stopped and grinned.

"What's so funny?" Joanne said.

His grin widened. "It's not exactly the sort of thing you talk about when you're trying to impress someone."

"Ah," Trixie said, "so you are trying to—"

"Trixie!" Joanne warned.

Trey held out his hands. "You expected me *not* to try to impress you—both?"

"Points for honesty," Trixie said. "But, did you really think these guys had figured out immortality?"

Trey thought about it. "Sorry to say, but, yeah. It sounds like an obvious sucker story when I tell it, but at the time … well, all I can say is that this Ewen guy, if that's even his real name, is one cool character. I'm telling you, he had me convinced that I had to work hard to let me in on the game."

"He made you desperate to throw your savings at him," Trixie said.

"No," Joanne said. "That *does* makes it sound like a sucker story—"

"Look," Trey said, "there's no use in dancing around the truth. It is indeed a sucker story."

"And Ewen—that's his name, right? —sounds like a master at making any of us into suckers."

"I think you're patronizing me," Trey said, "and thanks."

"It's for Joanne's sake."

∞

Earlier, before Joanne came back from work, Duncan came by again. Trixie seemed surprised at first, but then said, "I'm glad you stopped by, Doctor Fenster. The infection seems to have actually gotten worse."

Even I could see that the redness had deepened and spread out from the small burn area.

"I'm not surprised," he said, washing his hands in the kitchen. "This often happens," he explained, walking back as he dried his hands with a paper towel, which I noticed he slipped into his coat pocket. "The antibiotic regimen must take its course." While she sat on the sofa, he carefully pressed his thumb around the perimeter, eliciting a yelp and little jerk from Trixie. "Yes," Duncan said extracting the tube from his coat, "looks like we caught it just in time."

Trixie squirmed and winced as he slowly rubbed on a new coating of cream.

At the door, he stood, just looking at her.

"Um," she said. "Thirty dollars?"

He nodded, watching her face until she handed him the money.

He turned to go, but she said, "Uh, wouldn't it make sense just to leave the cream with me? I could, like, maybe buy it?"

He looked at her and scrunched his brow. "I wish I could. I really do. But, you see … this is a new formula, not FDA approved yet."

"So, that means you can't leave me any? I mean, it looks like the tube is almost empty anyway."

He pursed his lips and shook his head. "No. Sorry. I could get into real trouble."

She sighed. "Okay, then. Thanks again."

He nodded and walked away.

She closed the door and just stood there. She looked down at her thigh, lightly touched it, and cried, "Ow! Damn, that hurts."

She saw me peeking around the corner. "Don't even think about licking it," she said.

I assume she didn't think I understood her.

But now the ferret brain wanted to lick it.

∞

Dresser. Finally, something momentous to report. Is this what I do? Report? Like a lieutenant returning with his platoon from a reconnaissance mission? If so, who exactly is the enemy, and what is the reconnoitered territory? Or, perhaps, more like a graduate student updating experimental results? And, if so, who, or what, is the subject, and who or what the control?

I don't really expect answers from you (you?), just as Joanne doesn't expect an answer from me when she holds up two colors of lipstick and asks which one matches her blouse.

After last night's dresser report, Joanne returned from her date with Trey and found Trixie lying on the sofa holding a bag of frozen peas on her thigh. "The microwave would be quicker," Joanne quipped, but the pained look of rebuke on Trixie's face sobered her. "It's gotten worse?"

"No," Trixie said, wincing. "I'm just angling for pity."

Joanne sat on the sofa at Trixie's feet and placed her hand gently on her friend's ankle. "Maybe you should get help?"

"I have, remember?"

"The doctor that stopped by? Foister?"

"Fenster. Doctor Fenster."

"Is he really a doctor? I mean, with a degree and all?"

"Joanne, I told you. He was our family doctor when I was a kid."

"I know. But, I mean, he carries a tube of antibiotic cream around in case he runs across a stray infection?"

"Why not? It's a handy thing to have on hand. Besides, it's still experimental."

"That would make him want to carry it around?"

"I don't know. Sure. Look, what's your point?"

Joanne shrugged. "It's just a little weird that a doctor makes two house calls in a row. Doctors don't do that anymore! If you don't cycle through their front desk, they don't get paid."

Trixie didn't look at her. She was flipping the tie strings of her shorts back and forth.

"Did you *pay* him?" Joanne said.

Trixie twiddled her tie strings and shrugged.

Joanne sighed. She shook her head and said, "See you in the morning, girl," as she stood up. "Wake me if you develop gangrene and find maggots."

"Thanks!" Trixie called after her. "That's an image to fall asleep to!"

The next morning, Trixie was still asleep on the sofa when Joanne left for a meeting at her office. When she came back, Trixie was awake, but still on the sofa.

"Didn't you have a shift this morning?" Joanne asked.

"I called in," Trixie said. "It could be lethal."

Joanne looked at her quizzically.

"After an hour on my feet," she explained, pointing at her thigh, "I'd be forced to kill myself."

Joanne came over and looked. "It's definitely gotten worse," she said, throwing Trixie a critical bent brow. "Look—the red area has grown. This infection is spreading."

Trixie sighed. "If Doctor Fenster doesn't come by noon, I'll go to urgent care."

"Why wait?"

She shrugged.

"Come on," Joanne said. "I'll drive."

Trixie shook her head. "I'll wait."

"Why? His magic cream doesn't seem to be doing the job."

Trixie shrugged.

"It can't be the money. You're paying him."

"Yeah, thirty dollars. Do you know how much it could add up to if I go to urgent care?"

"You've already given him sixty dollars. Today will make ninety."

"Exactly. I'm already invested."

Joanne stared at her. "It seems to me you're putting way too much trust in this guy."

Trixie thought, and then nodded. "That's exactly it. I trust him."

"Because he was your doctor when you were a kid? You know perfectly well that children can be susceptible to unearned trust in adults."

"What are you saying?"

"That you have loyalties to this guy simply because he was a unique care-giver when you were young."

"That's the point. He was unique."

"Because he provided care that your parents—your family—couldn't."

"No. It was more than just being a doctor. He's truly special. His passion, and com-passion, for people was legendary. I never told you how our family ended up with him in the first place?"

Joanne shook her head.

"When I was, I don't know, maybe six, my parents took me to our then-family doctor for some vaccine booster shots, and I suddenly realized that I was deathly afraid of needles. That was a real problem, because, believe it or not, I wasn't exactly a sweet-tempered child—"

"No!" Joanne exclaimed in mock amazement. "There was a time when you weren't a gentle angel?"

"Very funny. Anyway, as soon as I saw the needle in the doctor's hand I went berserk, kicking, screaming, even biting. My parents tried to calm me down, the doctor's assistant tried, and finally, the doctor suggested we try another time. We came back a week later after what seemed like hours of persuasion—brain-washing, really— from my folks. But I was evil. I pretended that I wasn't afraid now, and I waited until the doctor was about to apply the needle before I literally exploded—"

"Sorry, but you didn't literally explode."

"No. I did. My arms and legs flailed around like the Warner Bros' Tasmanian Devil."

"That's not literally exploding."

Trixie rolled her eyes.

"Sorry," Joanne said. "Pet peeve. Please continue."

"Anyway … I was so aggressive, I caused the doctor to stick the needle into his own stomach."

"You're kidding!"

"I wish. He was so mad, he told my parents that they should find another doctor for me."

"And that's how you came across Doctor Fenster?"

"He was amazing. My parents told him about my last meltdown, so he was ready. When I *exploded*, he leaned back, and stood there smiling, with his arms crossed, as though enjoying the show. This made me angry, and I started screaming. He just stood there watching, and, I don't know, something in his smile told me that, while my behavior was totally out of line, he wasn't going to let it get to him. But, at the same time, it said that, once I decided to let the tantrum go, we could be friends. I don't know. It was weird. But it worked."

"You let him give you the shot?"

"Oh no. I wasn't ready for that yet. No, he led me off to one of the examining rooms. He said I must be tired after all that exercise, and it would be good to rest awhile. Then he closed the door, and left me all by myself. I wasn't afraid, but I was … maybe lonely? I sort of, I don't know, put things in perspective. After about ten minutes, he opened the door just enough to stick his head through and asked if it was all right for him to come in. You see? He asked me."

"So, at that point, it was your choice."

"Exactly. He sat on his stool in front of me, and said that, in fact, he didn't like to get shots either. They did hurt a little. But he said that he got his anyway because he knew they helped him from getting sick. Now, this was a revelation. *Doctors* got shots? And to prove it, he swabbed his arm, and gave himself a shot, right there in front of me. He gave a little wince and said, 'Yep, she stings a little bit.'"

"He gave himself the *vaccine*?"

"No. It must have been saline solution or something. Well, what could I do at that point? I think if he'd said,

'See? That didn't hurt' instead, I wouldn't have trusted him."

"So you got the shot?"

"Of course. What kind of story would it have been otherwise?"

Joanne sighed and nodded. "He does sound special." But then she glanced down at Trixie's thigh. "Damn, girl! That sure looks nasty." She shook her finger at Trixie. "He'd better be here by noon."

"Or what?"

"I'll lock you in the bathroom for ten minutes to put things in perspective. And then I'll drag you off to urgent care."

That was not the Duncan I had encountered in the alley. I thought that this was perhaps a different Duncan, but I had seen him clearly from my hiding places. Trixie wouldn't have mistaken him. It had to be the same man.

Noon came and went, and Joanne was standing in front of the sofa, fists on hips ready to argue, when the doorbell rang. She walked over and opened the door to reveal Duncan standing there a little surprised. "I'm, uh, here to see—"

"Trixie," Joanne said, standing aside to let him in. "You must be Doctor Fenster. She's gotten worse," Joanne said, following him to the sofa.

"Let's take a look," he said, starting to kneel down.

"Would you like to wash your hands?" Joanne said.

"Of course," he said quickly, standing up. "I just wanted to get a first look."

Joanne glanced quickly at Trixie, who shrugged.

"Hmm," Duncan said when he came back and peered at the wound.

"Bad, huh?" Joanne said, looking over his shoulder.

He pondered. "It's running its course okay," he declared, reaching into his coat for the tube of cream.

"Doctor Fenster," Joanne said, "are you serious?"

He looked up at her, his ruddy face turning a darker shade. "Are you a doctor?" he asked.

"No … of course not—"

"Then could you please let me handle this?"

"Um, sure. I'm sorry. I just think that it seems to be spreading—"

"You're blocking the light. Will you please step away?"

Joanne looked at him, and then walked around to the back of the sofa.

"A couple more days should do it," he said, unscrewing the cap to the tube.

I had been hiding behind a chair, and I moved softly closer, hiding among Trixie's spread of possessions. Duncan held the tube in his closed hand as he squeezed a little onto his finger. I caught a glimpse of a label, but not enough to see what it was. Ferret instinct urged me to find a deep dark place to hide from this man who had trapped me in the alley. My sense of duty to Joanne, and, by connection, with Trixie, however, took me stealthily around the coral reef towards the door. Why, I wasn't sure.

Trixie moaned when he rubbed the cream on her wound, and I could see that she was struggling to keep still.

Behind the sofa, Joanne had been doing pushups with her toes, where she repetitively lifted her heels off the ground, her hands clasped before her. I'd seen her do this while waiting for a call back from Craig. "Doctor," she suddenly said, "I'm really sorry, but I'm scared."

He glanced up at her and then grunted as he got to his feet. "There's nothing to be afraid of. These types of infections look like they're getting worse at first, but the cream is doing its job."

She looked at Trixie, but her friend had closed her eyes against the pain. "It wouldn't hurt to go to urgent care."

"No!" he snapped, and then seemed to compose himself. "She needs to remain immobile."

"Why?" Joanne said.

He looked at her, as though trying to burn a hole through her head with laser vision. "Because I said so. And I'm the doctor, remember?"

They glared at each other, a silent mental battle. "Trixie!" Joanne finally said without taking her eyes from Duncan. "Come on. We're going."

Duncan's jaw muscles worked, like kittens playing under a sheet. "Trixie, you are to remain immobile until I come back tomorrow," he said through clenched jaws. "Do you understand?"

She finally opened her eyes, but her face remained pinched with pain. She looked up at Joanne, and then at Duncan, and nodded.

Joanne snorted in frustration.

"Thirty dollars," Duncan said perfunctorily, holding his hand out.

Joanne stared at him as Trixie, with little grunts and moans, took her wallet out of her purse, looked inside it for some seconds, and then pulled out two bills, which she handed to him.

He looked at the two twenties and pushed them into his pocket as he turned to go.

I knew enough about aggressive infections to realize that Trixie could lose her leg. Worst case, she could die from septic shock. I don't know how I knew this, but I did. This Duncan was the same Duncan that tried to hack Schoeman, the crippled teen's father, in the back with an ad hoc ax. This was a Duncan that neither Trixie nor Joanne really knew. I also understood that harm to Trixie was harm to Joanne. And, besides, I had grown fond of the irascible woman.

Predictably, the thought of what I was about to do set me shivering. I tried not to think about the dreams to come. I crouched low, and launched myself up, onto the little table that sat next to the door. The surface was smooth, and I knocked Joanne's keys off with a clatter as I scrambled to pull myself fully up. When I turned, Duncan was standing there, eyes wide. I shouted, "This man is a fraud!" It came out as a snarling hiss. I closed my mouth, and sat up straight and calm, mimicking the ancient Egyptian statues of cats.

Duncan stared, frozen like a statue himself.

This in itself wasn't going to provide anyone a clue about the man. I felt myself growing faint at the thought of what I needed to do. This would be crossing a line. A line so serious, I might not survive.

So be it. I decided that living as a puppet wasn't worth living. Or, at least this is what I tried to bravely convince myself. Leaning back against the wall for support, I lifted my two front paws, and placed them on my neck. I felt my vision fading, and shook my head, fighting the embedded reaction. When my view cleared, I saw that my message had been received. Duncan clearly understood that I was referring to the vile collar he had made from his belt, for he had staggered back a few steps and his eyes were deep wells of horror.

His head snapped to the side, towards Joanne and Trixie. "Schoeman put you up to this!"

The two women were staring, confused. Joanne slowly shook her head. She opened her mouth to speak, but closed it again.

Duncan staggered back another step and bumped into the coat rack. "What in God's name more do you want from me? I *said* I was sorry!" His head shot back to me, as though confirming that I was real, and then again to Joanne and Trixie. "Do want a pound of flesh? Would that finally do it?" He glanced at me yet again. "Maybe you'd like this little demon to gnaw it out of me?"

His eyes grew even wider—a seemingly impossible feat—and Duncan suddenly sprang for the door. He yanked it open, took one last look at Joanne and Trixie, then at me, which caused me to cower, and, leaving behind a little squeal, he was gone.

Time floated, suspended. Cautiously, as though wary that he might burst back through the doorway, Joanne came and closed the door. She flipped the lock. I jumped to the floor and waited, shivering, not sure what she would do. She looked down at me in wonder, and my vision began to fade. Through the fog of mental attack I saw her open her mouth, but close it again. She blinked, dazed, and then seemed to wake from a troubled sleep. She threw her gaze to Trixie. "Get up. We're going to urgent care."

She started towards the sofa, but paused, bent over, and picked something up. It was the tube Duncan had been using. She uncoiled it, and stared at the label. Her face contracted in concern, but then opened in mirth. She held it up for Trixie to see. "It's Neosporin! You can buy this at the checkout line in the supermarket."

∞

At urgent care, they gave Trixie a wide-spectrum antibiotic shot, and sent her home under Joanne's supervision. For the rest of the day, she was to take Trixie's temperature every half hour, and check whether the red area was expanding outside a border they marked with a Sharpie. If either indicated a spread of the infection, she was to take Trixie to the emergency room.

As of now, 8:00 PM, Trixie seems to be responding to the antibiotics, but Joanne plans to check on her every hour through the night.

Once Joanne had Trixie comfortably ensconced back on the sofa, she turned to me, and I felt the trembles begin. She lifted me onto her lap and looked into my eyes. "Rascal," she said, "what did you do?"

I returned her probing gaze steadily, fighting the urge to look away. She was asking as though she actually expected me to answer somehow. I tried to act like a normal ferret, but the incessant shaking made that difficult.

"What's going on in that little brain of yours?" she whispered, her gaze searching and mesmerizing.

I wondered if I should just give up and try somehow to communicate, sentience-to-sentience, but this thought, fleeting as it was, set me to shaking so violently, she had to tighten her hold to keep me from falling off her lap.

She sighed and pulled me to her, wrapping her arms around me so that my head was buried in the crook of her neck. "You're something special, all right," she said softly.

I know that I am, and it was good to be told.

Chapter 6

Okay, I give up, dresser. I'm back. As I'm sure you know, after horrendous hours of nightmares two nights ago, I was too dazed and tired to report here. On second thought, since I am talking to you with my thoughts, you may well know *all* of my thoughts. No use trying to hide anything, I guess. I was indeed too tired yesterday to do or see anything to report on, but mostly I didn't come out of anger. Can you blame me? You torture me for simply helping my host. I understand that you don't want my intelligence to be revealed, but what would you do if you were in my shoes? Or, I guess, my paws?

In any case, nothing to report today. Again, as you must know, last night I was determined not to sleep, but by early morning I was not able to resist, and you slammed me with the most gruesome scenario—seconds, it seems, after I fell asleep.

Look at it this way, if you continue to punish me by ruining my sleep, you will eventually degrade my health, perhaps leading to an early demise. I must be an investment of some kind. Don't you want to protect it?

∞

No nightmares last night. Was it my logical argument, or simply that I behaved yesterday? I suspect I'll find out in time.

Joanne has not been talking to Trixie for the last half hour, and it has made for an uncomfortable household, considering that Trixie's "bedroom" is the center of the apartment. Trixie lies there on the sofa reading, surreptitiously glancing at Joanne every time she walks past. All she has to do is apologize to Joanne, but she insists she did nothing wrong. In my opinion, it was Joanne's fault for letting Trixie near her parents again.

Let me explain. Joanne had invited her parents over for dinner to celebrate their thirtieth wedding anniversary. She decided to take a big step and invite Trey … to meet her parents. Since she chose not to send Trixie off for the evening, her friend received a de facto invitation.

Joanne had told Trey that her parents were on the conservative side, but in retrospect she wished she had been more emphatic. During dinner, the conversation rolled around to Trixie's urgent care visit. "My co-pay was twenty dollars," she said. "The coffee shop doesn't provide insurance, so I'm lucky I qualified for subsidies."

The table was silent. I have the sense that there are certain subject categories that comprise the battleground between the country's divide. This territory is a demilitarized zone, where each side exists in a state of ready-alert, hypersensitive to any infraction.

Trixie looked around, and Joanne gave her a warning glance, which she ignored. "You know," Trixie said, "everybody says that the healthcare system is broken, but I say the machine is purring along in tip-top shape."

Joanne's father glanced darkly at her. He was ready for an enemy volley.

"Yesaree," she said, imitating a redneck accent, "you just have to put it in perspective. Healthcare is a business, and by any measure the most successful one in the country. The insurance company executives and stock holders are happy as pigs in the mud."

Joanne's father cleared his throat, and resettled himself in his seat.

"Insurance companies enjoy a captured market," she continued. "They've got you by the balls. God help you if you don't have insurance."

Joanne's mother frowned at the language.

"You know," Trixie said changing to a conspiratorial tone, "I got the gal at urgent care to tell me what my bill would have been if I'd just walked in with no insurance. Take a guess."

Joanne was shaking her head. "Trixie, nobody wants to guess—"

"Trey," Trixie said, "take a guess."

Joanne looked at him a little panicky. Trey seemed completely clueless to the explosive charge about to ignite. "Hmm," he said gamely, "oh, I'd say between a hundred and a hundred-fifty."

"Ha!" Trixie crowed. "See? The general public has no idea what's going on behind the curtain. Eight—hundred—and—seventy-five dollars," she enunciated. "For one shot of antibiotics. My insurance will pay the contracted price of a hundred-eighty. You see? If you don't have insurance, you're f—"

"Trixie!" Joanne scolded.

Trixie looked at her. "Ucked," she finished. "Trey," she said, "do you see a solution? What about this Medicare-for-all?" she said, as though it was the most hair-brained idea she'd ever heard.

Joanne's look seemed to be pleading that he change the subject.

"Well," he said thoughtfully, "I wouldn't discount it out of hand. Nobody's going to get healthcare for free. I guess we either pay for it with our insurance premiums, or our employers' profits, and indirectly our wages. We'd have to make all that up in higher taxes, but I guess the goal would be that this wouldn't amount to more than what we're already paying."

Joanne's father put down his fork. "You're advocating socialism?" he said.

Trey tilted his head, a polite gesture of dissent. He obviously didn't catch the rumbling thunder. "Socialized medicine, I guess. Socialism sort of implies a broader reach."

Trixie was watching him, using her forearm as a crutch for her chin. Joanne had closed her eyes and let her forehead fall into her upturned fingertips. "And then we'll be waiting in line for hours to see an incompetent doctor who doesn't give a damn about you," Trixie said.

"That may be the case for, like, Romania," Trey said, "but almost all industrialized countries have a workable version of socialized medicine—the EU, Canada, Japan, Korea. In Australia, they even call their socialized system Medicare. And, surveys show that most people are happy with their care—"

"Wait!" Trixie said, her eyes wide with alarm. "You want to take the best healthcare in the world and throw it in the trash?"

"She's baiting you," Joanne said without looking up.

He didn't seem to hear. "Now, wait a second. I never said we should jump right into this without careful consideration, but you have to look at the facts. America may have the best medical research programs, and the best care for those that can afford it, but if you have the cheapest level of, say, an HMO program, you're not going to get timely access to—"

"Enough!"

It was Joanne's father. He picked up his fork and pointed it at Trixie. "We all see what you're doing here—except him," he added, tilting the fork towards Trey. "It's insulting, and you should be ashamed of yourself."

Trixie furrowed her brow in concentration and nodded enthusiastically.

"Go to hell," Joanne's father muttered as he attacked his food as though it was resisting.

Trey looked as though he'd been impaled.

∞

I don't know how much time I have, dresser. The world has turned upside down. We are prisoners, and it doesn't look good. Duncan has managed to send me spinning yet again.

Joanne answered a knock on the door to find him standing there. She tried to immediately close it, but he called out, "Wait! I need to talk to you! I'm … I'm so sorry about what happened."

Trixie sat up from where she was napping on the sofa. "Did you come back for your Neosporin?" she said.

He held up his palms. "Like I said, I'm so sorry. I need to talk to you—both of you—about that."

Joanne looked at Trixie, who shrugged, and then opened the door wide and stepped aside. "We could have contacted the AMA, you know," Joanne said, ushering him to a dining table chair.

He took off his aging jacket and draped it over the back of the chair. "That would not have done any good," he said, easing himself into the chair.

"Would you like to bet?" she said. "That was complete and utter negligence. The urgent care doctor said that if we hadn't gotten her in that very day—"

"No, you don't understand. Contacting the AMA would have been appropriate if I were actually still a member."

Silence. "How could you *not* be a member?" Trixie asked. "I thought you had to be in order to practice medicine—"

"You do. That's the whole point. I was disbarred ten years ago."

"That means," Joanne said carefully, "that we could have actually called the police."

Duncan took a breath and nodded. "I can explain. And it's not easy."

Joanne sat down at the table across from him, and Trixie pushed herself up and limped over as well.

"I have a problem," Duncan began. He stopped, staring at his folded hands on the table. "This isn't easy."

"You came to us," Joanne said gently but carefully.

"Yes. Of course. Okay, here goes." He looked up and into their eyes. "I am an addict."

Joanne and Trixie blinked.

"An opiate addict, to be precise," he said, "and I made a terrible mistake ten years ago, a mistake that nearly ruined—has ruined—a young girl's life."

He lowered his eyes.

"That's what got you disbarred?" Joanne asked.

He nodded without looking up.

"You were leading Trixie on because you needed money—for your fixes."

He didn't answer, just stared at his hands.

"That's obvious," Joanne said. "If you can't even admit that, then there's no reason—"

"Yes!" he said looking up at them. "I live in a hovel, and nearly all of my social security goes to my habit. There are days when I don't have money to eat."

Joanne watched him, waiting.

He sat there, staring.

"Doctor Fenster," Joanne said patiently, "what do you want from us?"

He looked at her and took a deep breath. "I'd like you to come with me to an NA meeting."

Joanne glanced at Trixie. "You'd like me to come with you? Why?"

"Both of you. Why. That's a good question. The answer is embarrassing—no, shameful. This will be the fourth time that I'm trying. The last three times ..."

He seemed to drift off someplace beyond them.

"Doctor Fenster?" Joanne said.

He shook his head. "I couldn't do it. I didn't even make it through the first meeting." He hung his head. "Pride, I guess."

"You also have a debilitating habit," Joanne reminded.

He looked at her.

"I mean, your addiction was fighting for its own life."

"Weak," he said, hanging his head again. "Shameful."

The three of them sat there in silence. Joanne looked at Trixie. "Well?"

"Through his selfish disregard for the barest sense of responsibility," Trixie said, "he caused me to almost lose my leg. Sure, I'm game."

Duncan had looked at her in alarm, but his face relaxed when he realized she was toying with him.

"Okay, then," Joanne said, placing her hands palms-down on the table, "when is the next meeting?"

"This evening," he said.

"This *evening*? You expect us to just drop everything at a moment's notice?"

He looked pained. "I know. It seems irresponsible—it *is* irresponsible. It's just …"

"You're afraid you'll change your mind," she said.

He looked at her, and then nodded.

Joanne turned to Trixie. "Can you hobble to the car?"

"I'll skip and do cartwheels."

When the other two gazed at her quizzically, she reached out and placed her hand on Duncan's. "Doc, I remember how you helped me as a kid. I think that guy's still in there."

His eyes glistened with tears, and he abruptly stood up. "Well, then," he said, wiping his sleeve across his face. "I'll meet you there at seven. It's at the Methodist church over on Maple."

After he left, Joanne said, "Good Lord, what have we gotten ourselves into?"

"Heaven, I presume," Trixie said. "God damn, it had better."

∞

From what I gathered listening to Joanne and Trixie later as they whispered together, this is how events transpired. They'd been expecting a meeting lasting perhaps an hour, but upon arriving and hooking up with a very nervous Duncan, they found, to their annoyance, that there would be a presentation by a rehabilitation specialist afterwards, and Duncan insisted that they stay for the entire event. After looking at each other skeptically, Trixie had placed her hand on Duncan's shoulder and said, "We said that we'd be here for you, and by damn, you can count on us," to which he teared up again.

They walked inside, and paused before a circle of people sitting in chairs, mostly talking and occasionally laughing, but a few silent and morose—the ones Joanne assumed were struggling. There were only two empty chairs together, so Duncan, somewhat reluctantly, took a chair by himself, and settled in to become one of the morose people. After two of the members gave their updates, the chairperson called on Joanne, assuming that she was a new member. "Um," she said, flustered, "I'm actually here to support, uh ..." She looked at Duncan, who raised his hand and stood up.

"My name is Duncan, and I am ..." He sighed. "I'm an addict."

After the group acknowledged and welcomed him with careful grace, he looked around and continued, "This is my fourth attempt to kick my addiction." He paused, wiping the palms of his hands on the front of his pants. "This time, with the help of my friends ..." here, he gestured at Joanne and Trixie, "I intend to see it through."

He waited for the polite applause to end. He scanned the group again, as though deciding. "I was once a doctor—what I mean is, I was once a doctor licensed to practice medicine. My addiction stole that from me." He nodded, agreeing with what he'd said, seeming to gather steam. "Twelve years ago, my college roommate moved to the city. We had always been rivals—in grades, in dating girls, and, of course, in sports. He suggested we meet for a game of tennis. I hadn't played in years, and in my determination to best him, I tore the rotator cuff—cartilage—in my shoulder. It was extremely painful, and my colleagues urged me to have surgery. I'm used to giving advice, not taking it. Instead, I prescribed myself light pain killers, and when that didn't cut it, opiates. We—doctors—aren't supposed to self-prescribe, and when I began to see raised eyebrows from my colleagues, I allowed another friend of mine to prescribe them for me."

He scanned the room, maybe looking for other addicts he might recognize. "You can obviously guess where this is going. By the time I realized—no, admitted—that I had a problem, the opiate hook was firmly planted. This doctor friend finally refused to give me any more prescriptions, and I turned to my sister and other friends. I would prescribe opiates for them, and they'd pass it back to me. This didn't last long, and in the end, I was getting it on the street. My performance was deteriorating, and I was losing patients. This, while my supply was becoming more expensive. My street suppliers knew I was a doctor, and quadrupled the price."

Here, he suddenly paused and turned his gaze to Joanne and Trixie. "In my desperation, my complete sublimation to the habit, I made a terrible, terrible professional mistake. I prescribed the wrong drug for a young girl. I convinced myself that she had an ailment different from what the symptoms were indicating. Unfortunately, the drug I prescribed actually progressed her disease, and—" His words caught in his throat, and he put his hand to his brow a moment. Gathering himself while the room patiently waited, he said, "She ended up crippled, crippled for life."

He struggled to continue, fighting the tears. "I did this," he finally said, breaking down completely, "because the drug manufacturer was paying me to push this new drug."

He buried his face in his hands and sobbed.

Joanne stood up and looked at the chairperson, who nodded. She went to Duncan and placed her hand lightly on his shoulder, and he immediately wrapped his arms around her neck, his shoulders heaving as he took deep breaths against the sobs. Trixie came, and for once just stood silently nearby.

He suddenly pulled away, gazing at Joanne and Trixie as though just realizing who they were. He shook his head emphatically. "I can't do this," he said, and started away.

"Duncan!" the chairperson called, but he held his hand up without looking back.

At the door he turned and waved for the two of them to follow. Outside the room, in the church foyer, he pulled a handkerchief from his pocket and blew his nose noisily.

"Doctor Fenster," Trixie said, "you know we're here to support you—"

He held his hand up as he finished blowing, and put the handkerchief back in his pocket. "No, wait," he said, his voice nasal-heavy, "I have to explain something."

He seemed to be searching for the words. "This was supposed to be a ruse."

He paused and looked slightly startled, as though surprised by what he'd said.

"I don't understand," Joanne said. "Leaving the meeting like that? Is that what you mean?"

He shook his head, impatient. "No. The whole NA thing. I've been paid to pull you here."

Joanne glanced at Trixie and shrugged. "Why?"

"I don't know," he said.

"You don't know? Somebody paid you to bring us here, and you don't know why? Who? Who wants us here?"

"I don't know that either."

Joanne looked at Trixie, who stepped in, "Doctor Fenster, are you all right?"

He looked at her, quizzically, and then seemed to understand. "I'm clear of mind. Let me explain. After I left your apartment the other day, I was approached by a man. He wouldn't give me his name. He said that he knew about me, that I needed money, and offered me three-hundred dollars if I would bring you here."

Trixie glanced at Joanne, a look questioning his sanity. "And you don't know why," Trixie said. She suddenly glanced around the empty foyer. "This man, he's, uh, here somewhere?"

"I don't think so. At least, if he is, I don't think he'll approach you."

"Why do you say that?" Joanne said, splitting her attention between the door to the meeting room, and the door from outside.

"It's pretty clear that it's the next meeting that he's targeting. He told me he'd give me one hundred if I got you away tonight, and the other two hundred after the next meeting. Do you see? He wants this evening to be sort of a dry run, perhaps to make sure I can do it."

"Of course," Joanne said, "if he *is* here watching, he may know now that you've bailed."

"Let's get out of here," Trixie said. She held out her arms. "See? Goosebumps."

Joanne bit her lip. "Yeah. We should leave."

Trixie nodded. To Duncan, she said, "You need a ride?"

"Oh, no. I'm going back in."

"You are?" Joanne said, surprised. "I thought this was all a ruse."

"It was," he said. "I'm going to give it another go, though." He grinned. "After all, I've lost the money for my next fix—I *have* to get clean, now."

Joanne looked at him a moment, and gave him a long hug. "You're a good man," she said and stepped back.

His eyes glistened with tears again. "I'm going to try," he said. He nodded, and went inside.

"Come on," Trixie said, heading for the outer door. "My goosebumps are about to pop."

∞

That's how the two of them ended up outside Joanne's door just thirty minutes after they had left to meet up with Duncan. After they'd left, I lay on the sofa and practiced breaking the sleep taboo. It was not easy, and I was not successful, but I keep trying. I refuse to willingly submit to being a puppet.

Although I was not able to fall asleep completely, I was drowsy enough to lose track of time, so that when my satellite-dish ears swung around at the sound of metallic scraping at the apartment door, I assumed it was Joanne and Trixie returning, and I trotted over to meet them. The scraping continued, though, as though Joanne had the wrong key, or was perhaps inebriated. I heard a man's voice, and, for a moment, thought that Joanne had arrived with a date, but then I heard another man say, "You said you could do this blindfolded." The first man told him to shut up and stop distracting him. I assumed that they'd come to the wrong apartment, when suddenly the door swung open. The ferret brain took over, and the next instant I was hiding under the little table next to the door.

"Hear that?" the first man said.

"What?"

"Rustling. Like a mouse."

"Hey, maybe it was a mouse."

"Very funny. Lock the door."

"Why?"

"Use your brain. Nosey neighbors could walk right in. You always lock the door behind you."

I heard the click as he flipped the lever on the door.

I recognized those voices, and then I got a whiff of Ewen, the man who had stolen Trey's bonus. The other one had posed as a city council candidate to draw Trey away.

"Ned," Ewen said, "sometimes I think Mom must have adopted you. Either that, or she was fooling around on Dad."

And now I knew the other one's name.

"Why?" Ned said.

"The fact that you have to ask why answers your question—"

"Here's the laptop," Ned said, flipping it open.

He'd walked to the table, and from there, he would see me hiding under the table if he looked my way. While he was occupied turning on the computer, I slunk out towards the back of the sofa.

"Hey!" Ned said, and I froze. "What the hell is that?"

They were both looking at me, Ned leaning over the table, and his brother looking on.

I dove behind the sofa, my nails sliding across the polyurethane-covered floor as Ewen said, "I think it's a ferret."

"It looked like a weasel," Ned said, coming halfway to the sofa and squatting down to peer under it as I looked under from the back side.

"A ferret is a kind of weasel," Ewen said. "Forget it."

"How did it get in here?" Ned said, putting his head sideways on the floor so that our eyes met. "Hey! I see him."

"There," Ewen said, pointing at my carry cage. "It's a goddamn pet. They must be a new fad—that's the second one in a week. Now focus," he ordered, sitting down in front of the laptop. "We don't have all night. Gimme the passwords."

Ned stood up, grunting, and pulled a folded piece of paper from his shirt pocket. He opened it and said, "Christ, there's, like, a hundred here."

"There's thirty-seven. Read them off."

Ned snorted. "You know, for two hundred bucks, you'd think they could categorize them or something. How many years do these go back?"

"How should I know? They don't come with a manual. Read."

Ned read off what seemed like random characters, and Ewen typed them. He shook his head. "Next."

"Where do they get them from?" Ned said. "I mean, how do we even know they're, like, hers?"

"It doesn't matter. It's all we've got. Next!"

"Uh, the next one says, 'rascal.' You want to skip it?"

Ewen was already typing. His eyes went wide, and he sat back. "That was it! We're in. See? Even hackers have reputations they rely on."

I felt humbled, but, also sheepish, since, in a way, I had been their entrance key.

Ned was looking over his shoulder. "Check her emails," he said, and his brother turned to give him a hard stare. "Sorry," Ned said. "I'm a little nervous. Eight million dollars is a lot of money."

That number sounded familiar, but I couldn't place it.

Ewen was working the mouse, stopping occasionally to read. "Here! A message from Bank of America telling her that her monthly statement is ready."

"Bank of America. All right! Go to their site."

Ewen shook his head in disgust. "Brains, remember? There's a link right here in the email. With luck," he said, his finger poised over the keyboard, "her laptop will have remembered the account password." He tapped the keyboard, and sighed.

"No luck," Ned said. "Back to the list?"

Ewen stared at the screen. He nodded.

After entering five from the list, Ewen pounded the table with his fist, and Ned leaned in to look. "What's it say?"

"We're locked out. They give you only so many tries."

Ned leaned in closer. "It says they sent an email."

Ewen worked the mouse. "Yeah," he reported. "They're letting us know what happened." He read some more. "Yeah, yeah, thanks a lot," he muttered, tapping the keyboard. "The account's locked for one hour."

Ned read over his shoulder. "They say that if you need immediate assistance, you can call that number."

His brother gave him another dead stare. I had the idea that this happened a lot. "Yeah," Ewen said. "You call that number to report a problem—like you think someone's trying to get into your account."

"Ah," Ned said. "I guess that wouldn't do."

"Gee," Ewen said with mock surprise, "you think so?"

While this debate was unfolding, I heard sounds out in the hall. Women's voices. This time I knew immediately that it was Joanne and Trixie.

"Hey!" Ned whispered. "Hear that?"

Ewen raised his hand for Ned to be quiet. He pointed towards the kitchen.

Through the door, I heard Trixie say, "What do you think?"

"I think we're being silly," Joanne said. "Whoever it is, he wants us at Duncan's next meeting."

"What if this person lied to him? What if it's actually *tonight*?"

"Here?" Joanne said. I could tell she was nervous. "Like, it was all a ploy to get us out of my apartment?"

In the silence, I could imagine Trixie raising her eyebrows and nodding expectantly.

The doorknob turned a tiny bit. "Whew," Joanne said, relieved. "It's still locked."

I turned to see what the two intruders were doing.

They had disappeared.

Chapter 7

The door opened, and Joanne poked her head inside. From behind her, Trixie said, "Any bad guys?"

Joanne shook her head and stepped in.

I came out from behind the sofa. I had to warn them. But how?

"Hey, Rascal!" Joanne said, reaching down to pick me up.

I scampered away, off to the table. I looked up at the open laptop, and back at Joanne.

"What's wrong with him?" Trixie said.

"He's a ferret, that's what's wrong with him," Joanne said. "Who knows what goes on in that little mind?"

This called for something drastic, and that thought beckoned panic at being revealed. I quashed the fear, or more accurately, tried to ignore it.

"I've had to pee for the last hour," Trixie said, walking to the bathroom. "All that talk about drinking at the meeting didn't help."

Steeling myself, I hopped up onto the chair, and then lifted myself up on my hind legs and placed my front paws on the edge of the laptop. This blatant display made me dizzy with apprehension, and I swayed, desperately hanging on to my sanity.

"Rascal?" Joanne said softly, cautiously, seriously. She walked over and looked at the computer screen. "That's odd," she said, leaning in to see. "Trixie!" she called. "Did you leave the laptop on—?"

From the bathroom came a shout from Trixie, followed by her muffled protests. A moment later, she appeared with Ewen behind her, one hand wrapped around her mouth, and the other holding a gun to her side.

Joanne stared, silently, eyes bursting with alarm.

Ned stole out of the kitchen, knife poised high. Joanne had her back to him, staring in horror at Trixie, who's eyes burst with warning at what was about to befall her friend. Trixie squirmed and shouted, but Ewen's hand filtered the words, rendering them meaningless.

It was up to me. I jumped to the floor, my muscle control so compromised that I stumbled towards Ned as though drunk. I could bite his ankle. I repeated this to myself, not entirely believing it. The veracity of my belief was made moot as Ned swung his foot in an arc, sending me rolling back into the living room. By the time I recovered and stood shakily on trembling legs, Ned was hugging Joanne from behind, his arm wrapped around her waist, as though whispering enticing suggestions into her ear. Then I saw that his other hand was holding the knife to her neck.

I could still bite his ankle ... which could cause him to cut her throat as likely as let her go. I sat on my haunches and waited.

"What'll we do?" Ned said, pressing the flat side of the knife blade against Joanne's neck to make sure she understood the situation.

"What we came to do," Ewen said. He jabbed the tip of the pistol barrel against Trixie's head to stop her from trying to tear his hand from her mouth. "This is lucky. Now we have the password." He gestured with the pistol towards the chair in front of the laptop and nodded at Joanne. "Sit down."

"I can't," Joanne said.

"Why not?"

"There's a knife at my neck."

"Let her go," Ewen said to his brother. "Go over near the door. If they try to leave, kill them."

Joanne sat down and looked up at him fearfully.

"Do what I say, or I shoot your friend."

"He won't do it," Trixie said, the words barely intelligible.

"Oh yes, I will. I've killed two men already. Another won't make much difference if I'm caught."

Joanne nodded, short jerks of absolute obeyance.

"Don't believe him!" Trixie mumbled.

"Fine," Ewen said. He nodded to Ned across the room. "Give me your knife."

"What are you going to do?" Joanne said.

"Demonstrate just how serious I am. You can do a lot of painful damage with a knife without killing."

"I believe you!" Joanne exclaimed. "What do you want me to do?"

"Weeny!" came Trixie's muffled cry.

"Log into your bank account."

Nodding exuberantly, she turned to the laptop and worked the mouse. She looked up at Ewen, confused. "It says I'm locked out."

"Try it anyway."

She tapped away at the keyboard, and looked up again, shaking her head. "I can't." She turned back to the computer and clicked the mouse a few times. "They sent an email. The account will automatically unlock in … uh, forty-five minutes—"

"I know."

"Then why did you tell her to log in?" Trixie's gagged voice said. She pulled his hand away. "Look, I'm not going to scream, okay? Your hand smells like bad cheese."

His eyes narrowed, and he stared at the top of her head, as though suddenly finding it hateful. I tensed, waiting for the explosion of gun fire.

He shoved her away, pointing the gun at her face. "One peep, and your friend will be cleaning splattered brains off the wall."

"Oh, that's not stereotypical," Trixie said.

"You want me to gag you? I can jam a dishrag in your mouth, and then tie a belt around your head—"

"I know what a gag is. Don't worry, I'll just stand here quietly."

He stared at her, waiting.

"Totally," she said.

"One peep," he warned, shaking the gun at her. He turned to Joanne. "What's the password?"

Trixie groaned. "That wasn't a peep," she said.

Joanne looked from Trixie to Ewen. "It won't do you any good for another forty-five minutes."

"So? Let's have it."

Joanne shook her head, brow furrowed. "You don't need it for forty-five minutes."

"So what! Give it to me!"

"It buys us forty-five minutes," Trixie said.

Ewen glared at her.

"I'm just being helpful," Trixie said. "Once you have the password, you don't need us anymore."

He looked at her, then at Joanne. "I wouldn't know if you lied until then anyway."

Trixie raised an eyebrow. "You just admitted that you were going to kill us."

"I did not. Shut up, already!"

"Trixie," Joanne said, "I'm scared."

"I know," Trixie said, "I'm scared too—"

"I mean, please shut up."

"Oh."

"Okay," Ewen said, waving the gun, "both of you—over on the sofa."

I had been sitting there in the living room the whole time. The trembling had stopped, and I could think clearly. Ewen followed the two women, passing me a couple of feet away. Thinking about it beforehand provides time for the built-in restraint to muster its neurological weapons. So I didn't. As Ewen's leg swung by, I let impulse have free reign. I lunged ahead and grabbed his ankle in my jaws. The success of impulse is often the result of luck. The heavy material of his pants filled my mouth so that the tips of my teeth barely scratched his skin. It was enough to elicit a quick kick, though, that sent me tumbling towards Ned at the front door.

"Kill that thing," Ewen said.

"Right here?" Ned asked, holding the knife in preparation as he looked down at me skeptically.

"Are you worried about messing up the floor? Just do it," Ewen said, turning his attention back to the women.

Joanne's face had hardened, and she sprang from the sofa and past Ewen, who tried to grab her arm, but she shook his hand away. She ducked under Ned's raised knife and scooped me up. "That's not going to happen," she said into Ned's face, his knife inches from her ear.

"But this might," Ewen said. He was holding the gun against Trixie's head.

She frowned. "This is becoming a habit. Look, just put him in his cage."

Joanne didn't wait for agreement, and moments later I was looking out through the cage door at her as she latched it. She met my eyes, and we both searched for connection. I blinked, and she blinked, her worried mouth turning up just a bit at the corners. Letting impulse fly again, I raised my right paw, and placed it flat against the wire mesh of the door. Joanne's furrowed brow relaxed, and her eyes opened wide with delight as she placed her finger against it from the other side. Girding myself for what was to follow, I made a slow, deliberate nod to her, and the delight in her eyes swelled.

Ewen barked an order to sit back down, jolting Joanne away from my cage, as the blatant display of sentience curled me into a whimpering ball.

When the storm jamming my senses abated, I heard Joanne say, "But, I don't *have* eight million dollars. I'm trying to tell you, that was a mistake, a false assumption by the reporter."

"Newspapers don't make that kind of mistake."

"Sorry, but this one did. I have, like, seven thousand dollars in my bank account."

"You spent a thousand already?" Trixie said, and everybody ignored her.

"Is this true?" Ned asked, walking over, abandoning his post.

"Yes!" Joanne insisted. "Why would I lie?"

"So that we'd give up," Ned said, his face turning red and his free hand balled into a fist.

"She may be telling the truth," Ewen said darkly. He could have been reporting a tsunami bearing down on them.

"The risk is supposed to equal the reward!" Ned exclaimed, nearly shouting. "That's what you always say!"

"I know what I always say!" Ewen retorted, each word louder than the previous. He started to say something else, but punched the air instead, pacing back and forth in front of Joanne and Trixie.

"The eight million was our ticket to get away!" Ned cried. "This was going to be the big one! The risk worth taking! We can't get caught after … this!" he said, gesturing at the sofa.

Joanne and Trixie exchanged alarmed glances. I could guess what they were thinking—was the big risk simply kidnapping, or … murder?

Ewen stopped pacing and pointed the gun into Joanne's face, his hand shaking. He swung the gun to Trixie, who sat up straight in defiance, but I could see one of her fingers trembling in concert with his.

He lowered the gun and glanced at his watch. "We'll know if we're fucked in thirty-five minutes."

Ned glanced at the door. "Maybe we should just bail. Now."

"Sure. And leave these two to ID us. How far are we going to get? How are we going to set ourselves up somewhere else?"

Ned stared at him, his mouth tight.

"So, we wait," Ewen said, grabbing a chair from the dining area and setting it in front of the sofa.

"And hope she's lying," Ned said.

Ewen looked at him as he sat down, and then at Joanne. "She'd better hope she's lying."

What did he mean by that? I thought. If they had eight million dollars, they could leave the country before they were caught? If not, they couldn't afford to leave witnesses?

This was bad. Very bad. Joanne and Trixie would have to make a run for it. Ned was pacing, and Ewen sat idly flipping the pistol back and forth in his lap in front of them. Would he really shoot? Risk having a neighbor call the police? Ned was the real problem. A knife was silent. That's how they would murder the two later. That is, *if* they murdered them. Of course they would. On the other hand, Ewen might shoot on impulse, he wouldn't have time to think through the consequences. Joanne and Trixie would have to jump up at exactly the same time. Maybe one of them could get to the door. What kind of odds are those? Practically guaranteeing that one of them would be sacrificed? Besides, how would they coordinate with Ewen sitting there staring at them?

My mind raced in frantic disorder. I had to calm down, at least enough to think straight, direct my attention elsewhere for a few minutes, maybe review the last hours.

And so, dresser, that brings you up to date. I know that I'm not sitting on the actual dresser, but you have always been essentially a metaphor.

Isn't that right?

Chapter 8

Dresser, the metaphor behind which hides my tormentors, I am exhausted. Exhausted and depleted. Events transpiring after the last report were enough unto themselves to defeat my last grain of energy, but you, the puppet masters behind the mental curtain, battered me mercilessly until I came to believe you actually want me dead.

But, no more.

I had concluded that it was ludicrous to expect Joanne and Trixie to make a mad dash for freedom. They couldn't, but I could. Ewen had wanted me killed, but only because I was a bother. Once locked away in my cage, he hadn't given me another glance. What harm could a pet ferret inflict?

Of course, that is a valid question. What could I do, once free? Maybe trot off to the nearest police station and use my pseudo-opposable paw toes to wrestle a pen and scratch out a message? Given a half hour, and an infinitely patient desk sergeant, I might scrawl something legible, perhaps purposefully misspelling a few words so that he won't suspect my true intelligence. The non-fanciful scenario would be that they'd immediately call animal control, and if I tried to demonstrate that I was intelligently playing a Lassie role, I had enough experience to understand that a moment later, I'd be sprawled on the ground, catatonic. And then they might think I died, and toss me in the garbage bin.

All that would have to wait. First, freedom, and then how to capitalize on it.

My cage was in full view. I was looking at Ewen's back, but Joanne and Trixie were facing me, and Ned, pacing back and forth, might see me on one of his transits. I'd have to chance Ned, and—somehow—convince the other two to ignore me.

I slowly reached my paw out and down to the latch. As I pulled on the lever, it made a slight clang, and I jerked back as Joanne and Trixie looked. Neither Ned nor Ewen seemed to have noticed.

Trixie turned her attention back to Ewen, but Joanne continued to watch me. I'd have to do it. I could only hope that the resulting shut-down would last just a short time. I raised one paw, as I had done to meet her finger on the cage door. She grinned a little, tickled at my innocent pet gesture, nothing more than a cat might do. My paw began to tremble as I contemplated the next moves. Slowly, purposefully, I waved the paw back and forth. Her grin melted, and her brow contracted, and that change, that recognition of odd behavior, made me dizzy. I dropped my foot, swaying on all fours, but hanging on to consciousness.

When my vision cleared, Joanne was thankfully still watching. I didn't think I'd survive the next move, but I pressed on. Slowly reaching my paw out and down to the latch, I met her transfixed eyes, and, taking a deep breath, I nodded once. My vision fuzzed, but I closed my eyes and willed the demons away. I opened them to find Trixie also now staring, astonished. Joanne surreptitiously grabbed Trixie's hand lying on the sofa and squeezed it while simultaneously throwing her a warning look.

"What are you two up to?" Ewen said, turning to follow their gaze, and Joanne proceeded to prove her mettle.

She gave Trixie a shove. "You can't leave well enough alone, can you?" she exclaimed.

Trixie looked at her, cautious, trying to understand. Importantly, Ewen had turned his attention back to them.

"Sometimes," Joanne said, shaking a pretend-angry finger at her, "you have to just let things go!"

Trixie's cautious gaze turned mischievous. She understood. "You should talk, girl," she said, almost gleefully. "I think you go out of your way to remain clueless!"

Joanne threw me a quick glance, my cue.

As they exchanged insults in their faux argument, mostly nonsense now, unbeknownst to Ewen and Ned, I undid the latch, swung the door open, and climbed out onto the table. Ned happened to glance my way and shouted, "Hey!"

The race was on. I hopped to the floor as Ned sprang for me. I tried to run away, but my nails slipped on the polyurethane surface, my bane in life, and Ned reached down to grab me. I twisted around and bit his hand. Hard. The mental storm settled in, but this time I funneled the oppressive energy into an enhanced fight-or-flight response, in this case, flight, since I wasn't sure I'd weather another bite. Ned cursed me and sucked on his bleeding hand, and I gained enough traction to make it to the kitchen.

Praying that Ewen wasn't keen enough to go around the other way, I exited the kitchen out the opposite side into the hallway. There it was, the little swinging door next to the closet, still unlatched from my previous misguided exploration. I had bare seconds. I tried to pry the bottom of the door out, but couldn't get a purchase. I thumped the bottom with my paw, and the door bounced out a little. I thumped again, and this time caught the edge with my nose. Holding it in place, I lifted a paw and caught the inside edge with a nail so that I was able to swing the door open. As before, heady damp smells greeted me as I dove inside, and, as before, I let the bottom of the door slide along my back. In my excitement, I must have twisted, and the edge of the swinging door caught on my rear hip joint, leaving me dangling painfully upside down in the near darkness of the chute. I kicked my hind legs, trying to shake loose, but this just provoked more pain.

"Here it is!" said Ewen's angry voice.

My hind feet were suddenly squeezed together inside a strong fist, and the door opened, flooding the dank aluminum shaft with light.

I was done. I'd made a valiant effort, but I was done.

Suddenly, miraculously, my legs were free and I was falling as the world slammed again into darkness. Behind me as I fell, echoing within the narrow chimney, I heard Ewen shout, "You stupid bitch!"

Joanne or Trixie had apparently intervened.

Dim light rose to meet me, and my jaws chattered as I bounced on the soft pile of rubbish and rolled away, coming to a stop against the cold cement wall. For one irrational moment, I feared that Ewen would follow me down the chute, and then I relaxed, breathing heavily, recovering.

I heard rustling. Beady eyes were staring at me. A rat. A big one. The brother of the one I ate? I hissed, but the brute didn't flinch.

Shit.

I couldn't talk, but I could squeal. The rat had surely heard sirens, and wouldn't expect one down here. I opened my mouth and let go with my best interpretation of an ambulance, lacking heft from such a small throat, but amplified in the echoing room. I was impressed with my imitation. The rat was annoyed. I got to my feet and took a step towards him, imitating a police car. The rat backed away, not so much afraid, I think, as wary about complications tangling with something so clearly deranged. I tried an air raid siren as I backed in a circle towards the door, then turned and ran.

I froze at the opening, and the rat scampered away at the sound of men's voices coming down the hallway. "It sounded like a toy," one man said.

"What's it doing down here?" another man said.

"Some kid probably dropped it down the chute."

The ferret brain was desperate hide. I had escaped, not to hide, however, but to find help. The rest of my plan remained to be formulated, but help clearly implied people. My decision was resolved when I caught a glimpse of the two men. One of them was Trey's father, the man who had found me in the building's lobby.

I backed into the dark room and waited. The door swung wider, and they entered. I should have realized what would happen next, but I am not entirely in tune with thinking like a small mammal. I couldn't speak to get their attention, but I could squeal. "Holy Jesus Christ!"

the younger man shouted and kicked. His heavy work shoe caught me under the chest and sent me flying, again coming to rest with a thump up against the moldy cement wall.

Trey's father flipped the light switch and they both stood staring at me. Attempting to regain my dignity, I got to my feet, shook the loose debris from my fur, and looked up at them, unflinching.

"I know this critter!" Trey's father said.

"What is it?" the younger man asked.

"It's a ferret. Its owner lives in the building."

"How'd it get down here?"

Trey's father looked up at the opening in the ceiling and pointed. "It must have fallen."

"What'll we do with it?"

"My son knows where the owner lives."

"Um, close the door and leave it in here for the time being?" the younger man said.

Uh, oh. Time to be cute. I trotted over to Trey's father and sat looking up at him with my best lost-and-forlorn expression. He started to reach down, and I jumped into his arms.

"Looks like he's your problem now," the younger man said.

"It's okay," Trey's father said. "My son will know what to do."

Five minutes later, Trey's door opened, and his father pushed me into his hands. "Round two," his father said. "Can you deal with this? I've got to get back to a warped access door. Oh, and you might tell that gal to lock her garbage chute."

"Well," Trey said, carrying me high, away from a leaping, frothing Trump, "aren't you the little trouble-maker."

He put me in the cage on the bar separating the kitchen from the dining area, latched the door, and sat back down at his laptop. A minute later, he got back up, exclaiming, "Trump, if you don't calm down, I'm going to rip your tongue out!" He dumped the dog into his bedroom, closed the door, and said as he passed by, "I wouldn't actually rip his tongue out, but don't tell him."

It can be so confusing, and always the same—he said this as though he truly thought I understood.

Now I had to convince him that I might have, and the thought set me shivering. *Damn it*, I thought. I was getting so tired of the chains.

First, I had to get out of the cage, and that took all of twenty seconds. Trey sat with his back to me, and must have assumed the sound was just me poking around. What next? There was no way I was going to get him to go to Joanne's apartment without revealing the true me. I looked at the stove clock. Just six more minutes before Ewen would discover that Joanne had not been lying about her great-aunt's inheritance. My teeth began to chatter as I contemplated what I had to do. The more I envisioned it, the greater the storm winds howled between my ears, and the less control I had over my own muscles.

I'd had enough. Joanne and Trixie's lives were on the line. I couldn't go on like this. Anger, fear, and pure frustration overcame me, and I raised my snout and screamed, or, rather, squealed. I let it all go, feeling as though my intestines were dissolving away. And then I heard a pop—inside my head, like packaging cellophane giving way.

And I was free.

Fear had evaporated. Inhibitions disappeared. Trey had turned in his chair, and was staring at me. I tested my new untethered condition by raising my paw over my brow, like I was saluting him.

Nothing. I felt fine.

Trey was unsettled, though. His brow contracted, and he gazed at me, as if trying to understand if my gesture was some kind of fluke.

I had to be careful, I knew. Too much unnatural intelligence, and I would become a freak, a specimen to be studied.

And that meant being taken from Joanne.

I looked down, over the counter edge. Three feet is a long drop for a ferret. The kitchen side was tile, but the dining side carpet. Good enough. I jumped down, walked over, and looked up at the still-staring Trey. I nodded, a simple gesture, but his eyes expanded. I nodded again, and trotted to the door. I looked back, and he was still sitting, staring.

What would a dog do? I ran back to him, took a fold of pantleg in my mouth, and tugged, towards the door. I let go, went halfway to the door, and sat, looking at him.

His furrowed brow relaxed, and curiosity took over. "What are you up to, fella?" he murmured.

That was more like it. I got up, went to the door, and sat down, waiting, willing him to see the invitation in my eyes.

"You want to go out?" he said, getting—finally—up, and walking over. "You need to go potty?"

Potty? I wasn't a three-year-old. Actually, I was probably less than that, but that wasn't the point. I couldn't afford to defend my honor now, however, and went with it if that would get us outside. I turned to the door, lifted my foot, and placed my paw flat against it. Yeah, okay, I needed to go "potty."

"Hmm," he said, "no collar, which means no leash. You'll have to behave."

I wanted to stand up on my hind legs and do a little sarcastic dance. In fact, I started to, and had to scold myself that Joanne was waiting, probably with a gun to her head.

This mental freedom would take some getting used to.

Once outside his apartment, I started down the hall to the left, and he called to me. "Hey, bud," he said, pointing in the other direction. "This way."

That was probably the shortest way to get out to the grass, but Joanne's apartment was my direction. I sat, looked at him, and then got up, turned, walked a few steps, turned back, and sat again.

He thumped the heel of his palm against his forehead. "Of course! You want to go home … and you know the way." He started towards me, and I didn't wait. I trotted on ahead. He ran to catch up. "You're one smart little devil, aren't you?" he said.

I flinched out of habit, but there was no reaction to his recognition. I was free indeed. I picked up the pace. Joanne and Trixie were waiting.

I turned a corner, and stopped short. Trey came around and I jumped to the side to avoid getting stepped on. We were blocked by a policeman. He held keys, in the process of entering his apartment.

A policeman! Just what we needed. How could I get him to come along?

He gestured at me. "It's illegal to have pets off-leash," he said. He seemed tired, probably just getting off a shift.

Help had turned into a hurdle.

"Sorry, officer," Trey said, "it's actually somebody else's ferret. It got lost, and I'm taking it home."

We didn't have time to dally. I had to move this along. I stood up on my hind legs, and reached my front paws up to Trey. He bent down, and I jumped into his arms.

"Pretty tame," the policeman said. "I've seen you. You live here?"

"Yeah. Around the corner. Six doors down."

The policeman nodded. "See you around," he said, turning away and jiggling his keys towards the lock.

"Okay," Trey said, and walked on. He looked down, into my face. "You're quite the wiz kid. No wonder Joanne was so happy to get you back."

I let him carry me through the connecting hall to Joanne's wing, and on to her door. This was it. I'd gotten him here, but now what? He rang the doorbell and stepped back, waiting.

No one answered. What did I expect? Why *would* they answer?

"Sorry, buddy," Trey said, turning to go. "We'll try later."

No! I squirmed, twisting, and leaped from his arms, inadvertently scratching him and making him yelp. The floor hit me hard, and I got to my feet, shaking my head to clear it.

"Hey!" Trey said. "Sorry, bud, but Joanne's not home."

He reached down to pick me up, and I backed away, hissing. My rush of urgency had filtered down to the ferret brain.

"Whoa!" Trey said, taking a step back. "What's gotten into you?"

Things were getting desperate. What was the sound of desperation?

What, indeed. It was worth a try. *Anything* was worth a try.

I chose the police siren, and let loose. Trey's eyes went wide as he stood, frozen.

I wailed and wailed, my snout pointed at the sky. I wailed until my voice began to crack.

The door suddenly swung open, and Ned stood there, glaring, knife in hand. He looked at Trey, the wide-eyed statue, and down at me. "What the hell?" he said as I made for the opening. I saw his hand swing down, and a sharp, stinging pain jolted my hind quarters. I slid across the slippery floor, spinning slowly around as Ned slammed the door shut.

I had risked my life to get away, and now I had forced my way back for no rational reason. It wasn't about logic, just that I couldn't let a door come between Joanne and me again.

She sat at the laptop looking defeated, and Ewen stood over her, his pistol pointing at the ceiling. His face was flushed, and his eyes wild. "God-damned it!" he yelled. "God *damned* it to hell! What the *fuck!*"

I took the only action available to me—distraction. Ned came at me, knife held ready. I rose up on my hind feet, raised my paws, and growled. My rear leg exploded with excruciating pain, but the miniature grizzly bear imitation stopped Ned short as he absorbed the bizarre scene.

This was my ticket. Keep their attention and lethal weapons away from my friends. I turned and did a hand stand, so that the mesmerized Ned appeared upside down before me. Paws provide no base for balance, and I fell over backwards, generating enough pain in my hind quarter to blur my vision. When it came back into focus, Ned was swinging the blade down. I rolled, and heard a thud as the blade sank into the wooden floor.

Ned worked to free the knife, and this allowed me to exit into the kitchen. Distraction. It drove Joanne crazy when I made a racket while she was working. I hopped onto the little stool Joanne kept there, and up onto the counter, and then fell back when my right hind leg refused to cooperate. As I slid off the smooth laminate kitchen top, I caught my nails in the filigreed base of a bowl of fruit, pulling it off the counter to clatter to the floor. This provided enough leverage to next grab the toaster, which followed the bowl, crashing down to hang, swinging, suspended by its electric cord.

But I was up. Joanne kept a menagerie of pots and pans hanging from hooks under the cupboard. I had discovered their vulnerability just before Joanne not only locked me in my cage, but then deposited the cage in the closet for an hour. I ran under the line of pots, arching my back and lifting each one in turn off its hook. The cascade of clattering was deafening.

I turned to find Ned swinging his knife at me. It was a sideways swipe, reaching under the cupboard, and I ducked behind one of the larger fallen pots, which slammed me into the corner when Ned's knife-fisted hand made contact. Corners are not good places in a fight, and

I leapt over the pot to get away. That's what I attempted to do, it's what my brain told my hind quarters to do, but only one responded enthusiastically so that I fell, rolling off the pot. This may have saved me, for Ned's next jab landed where I would have otherwise. For one flashing instant, his wrist lay an inch from my head, and the ferret brain lunged, piercing the skin with my little teeth.

Ned yelped, and I was dragged across the counter as he pulled back his arm, causing more fallen pots to crash to the floor. His knife, still clutched in his fist, slid along beside me, and I wanted to ask the ferret brain what it intended to do now, but it was totally focused on clamping onto the aggressor.

I saw that I was about to be dragged right off the counter, and I let go, immediately scrambling to get away from the next knife swipe.

The swipe didn't come. Instead, Ewen yanked Ned aside, shouting, "Kill that goddamn thing already!"

"I'm trying!" Ned yelled back. "It's not easy!"

"Well, I've had it!"

I looked up, right into a dark hole, the barrel of his gun. I should have at least tried to move away, but I was paralyzed. The ferret brain hardly took notice, but I knew what a bullet would do, and fear gripped my heart. I would be dead now, but at that instant, his hand swung aside as the kitchen exploded with a blast louder than I had ever imagined. My head seemed stuffed with cotton from the sound concussion, and particle board dust rained down around me where the bullet had blasted through.

Joanne had pushed Ewen just as he'd pulled the trigger, and he now swung his arm, catching the side of her head with the pistol. She fell, and he aimed the pistol down at her, now out of my view. He swung the gun up at Trixie, who had been right behind her, and she backed away, both hands held high.

Ewen's face was twisted in outrage and frustration. I wondered why they hadn't run for the door. They could have been free, the whole point of my desperate antics. I had miscalculated, though. Joanne wouldn't run away and leave me. I was just a little mammal, but I was still her friend, and friends don't abandon friends.

Ewen, his mouth squirming with rage, turned the gun back on me. He was going to enjoy this, payback for my disruption. I didn't know what to do to save myself. I couldn't see any way out, so I took one last gesture of protest. I stuck out my little tongue at him.

He stared, surprised by the surrealism.

And that saved my life.

"Put it down!" a man's voice yelled.

It was a policeman, standing just outside the kitchen, holding his pistol in both hands, aimed at Ewen's chest. In the distance, but getting closer by the second, a police car siren wailed. Ewen looked at the cop's gun, and then at his face. The rage in his face gave way to angry despair, and he slowly laid his gun on the counter next to me. His gaze moved to his brother, who had laid his knife down as well. "You didn't lock the door, you stupid fuck."

It was the same policeman that Trey and I had encountered. In fact, Trey peeked around the corner. "I told you to wait outside," the cop said, throwing him a glance.

"Right," Trey said, taking it all in. "Like I was going to do that."

A groan rose from below the counter, and both Trixie and Trey rushed in to lift Joanne as the cop motioned for the other two to step into the dining area.

Joanne was holding her head and looked dazed. She saw me and smiled.

Trixie nudged her. "He stuck his tongue out at him. I think he gave him the finger as well."

That was not true. It's not possible for me to extend just one toe.

Otherwise I would have.

Chapter 9

"How'd he even know to look in your parent's local newspaper?" Trey asked, leaning forward from the backseat between Trixie, who was driving, and Joanne, who held me in her lap.

"Just luck, I guess," Joanne said, gazing fondly at me as she stroked my head with two fingers. "Luck for him, not me. Everything written is available, if you know what to search for."

"Unlucky for him in the end, actually. I guess the lesson is that you don't take any information that gets out there for granted, especially wrong information."

"And especially if the wrong information is off by three decimal points. I may not always have Rascal there to save me."

"Smart little guy, isn't he?" Trey said. "Did I hear Trixie say that he did a handstand in front of the guy with the knife? And then stuck his tongue out at Ewen with the gun?"

Joanne and Trixie glanced at each other. "She exaggerates," Joanne said.

"That's right," Trixie said. "The ferret is perfectly normal."

Her mastery at dry sarcasm is so developed, I don't think Trey even caught it.

"I don't know about normal," he said. "He practically took my hand to lead me to your apartment." He thought about it, and shrugged. "Maybe ferrets are just naturally smart."

"Indeed," Trixie said. "Some of them can even read and write."

My head snapped to look at her, but she looked at the road, smiling a little at her joke.

"This is it," Joanne said. "Turn in here."

I was surprised to recognize the building, even though I have no concrete memory of ever being there. The sign above the door read, "Twin Peaks Animal Clinic." It was the ferret brain's memory. Ever since the mental pop at Trey's apartment, the ferret brain's thoughts—as meager as they are—and memories have become more accessible, as though a mind barrier had dissolved. As Joanne carried me inside, I knew what the waiting area layout would be, and that the overpowering sweet smell was associated with the young woman at the check-in desk. She took off the cotton swap that Joanne had taped around my knife wound, and listened as Joanne explained that she had applied Neosporin—the same tube dropped by Duncan when he was still lost in his addiction. "It's not too bad," she said. "The doctor has two patients ahead of you. It should be maybe twenty minutes if you want to take a seat."

I expected Trixie to make a joke about animals being patients, but she just looked on, aware that Joanne was in no mood for levity while I was bleeding.

The young woman lifted my chin with her finger and looked me in the eye, and then frowned. She glanced up at Joanne, and recognition seemed to come to her. "Just one minute," she said, and left through a door behind her. Joanne looked back at Trixie and Trey, but they had picked up magazines, and were flipping the pages. The woman returned almost immediately, and said, "The doctor will see him right away." Without waiting, she gently picked me up.

"Um," Joanne said, "shouldn't I be filling out some forms?"

"Oh. Yes," the woman said. She shrugged. "We can do that later. Have a seat," she said over her shoulder as she carried me through the door.

We went down a short hall, and stopped in front of unmarked double doors, where she moved me to one arm in order to hold her badge against a sensor. The door made a small clunking sound, and we were through.

I was stunned to find that I recognized where I was. I scanned the large room, and suddenly found myself dizzy. This was the lab from my dreams—the man with the double chin, and the woman with a scar on her cheek shaped like a "T"—the motion Joanne makes when scolding me. The ferret brain recognized the place as well, and its response was anxiety. It was the overlaid memories—my own, and the ferret brain—that caused the dizziness.

"Well, well," the man said, taking me from her arms and laying me on the same examination table from my dreams. "Our wayward trouble-maker returns." He used his finger to pull down my lower jaw and peer into my mouth, and then pulled up my eyebrows to look at my eyes. "You in there?" he murmured.

"I doubt it," the scar-cheeked woman said. "We would have picked up tell-tales, but there was nothing."

"I know," the man said without looking up. "We need to make sure, though. We could buy this whole building for the cost of that HONIR."

I knew what a HONIR was. I hadn't a moment ago, but the information just appeared, seemingly out of nowhere. It stands for HOlistic Neuro-Inducer and Receptor, and it is a means to communicate and control—commune, essentially—with a brain. It is how I share this mind and body with the ferret brain.

Other information took shape out of the fog. I, the me thinking right now, am artificial intelligence implanted in this small mammal. Why? For no other purpose than to see if it can be done. Actually, that's not right. The whole project is the brainchild of one of the "dark" branches of the government—agencies that are not even acknowledged as such. Every year, congress funds over a billion dollars that disappear into developments so secret, even they have no idea where it goes. I am a ferret, more or less, to prove out highly-advanced technology that might one day serve our nation. Speculation in this lab is that it would presumably be used on spy or assassin assignments, but these scientists are not privy to that level of policy.

These were obviously memories that had been blocked—the reason that my existence seemed to begin when I woke in my cage that morning so many days before. That pop—I wondered if that wasn't some quantum level circuit that gave way under my mental tsunami. If so, I was probably now functioning in a way that was absolutely verboten by the dark powers that be.

"We'll need to autopsy the brain," the man said. "If we can't recover the HONIR, we at least need to know why it failed."

My ears swiveled. I knew what autopsy meant.

"You mean, confirm why it failed," she said, eyeing him.

"We don't know that it was the redirection dreams."

"I don't doubt that you don't know."

"You're already preparing your C-Y-A? You didn't exactly protest at the time."

"You're in charge, all I could do was express my doubts."

"Let's save the blame-game, and prepare for the autopsy."

"You're not thinking we'll do it now, are you?"

"Why not? Oh, yeah. The owner's right outside."

"We can't just tell her that she brought her ferret in with a small wound, and it died while we were bandaging it."

"I got that," he said, annoyed at being told what was already obvious. He stared at me, thinking.

"We give it telazol, and tell her that there's a small possibility of blood infection. If it's not acting normal, bring it back immediately."

He looked at her and nodded grudgingly, now annoyed that he hadn't thought of it. "She'll see it apparently become ill, and think it's the infection."

"I got that," she said, parodying him.

"In fact," he said, ignoring her dig, "we could over-dose it with slow-acting xylazine capsules. That way, if she fails to bring it back, it will at least be terminated."

"And we don't get that autopsy."

He shrugged. "Then we call in a special delivery."

"Oh, that won't get a lot of oversight attention," she said sarcastically.

He shrugged again. "Just covering our bases."

I could guess what a "special delivery" was—clandestine recovery of my corpse, by whatever means.

They sorted through their drug stock, and returned with a handful of capsules. The man first put a normal dose of telazol in my mouth, and rubbed my throat so that I would swallow, which I promptly pretended to do, and slid the slippery capsule back against my cheek instead. Next came three capsules of xylazine, which I also managed to stash away. These required special care not to burst, since apparently just one contained enough horse sedative to kill me. The woman then did a perfunctory job of bandaging my wound—without cleaning it, of course—and called in the front-desk woman to return me, along with the nefarious instructions, to Joanne, who thanked her, and wrote out a check. Nobody seemed to notice that one of my cheeks bulged as though from a massively infected tooth.

Once in the car, I squirmed off of Joanne's lap, and deposited the dire load under the seat. I looked at the saliva-slicked xylazine capsules. They could be dangerous if Trixie ever transported kids or pets who might find the drug delivery capsules interesting enough to ingest. I used my nails to puncture each one, then squashed them with my paw. I could apologize to Trixie later for messing her carpet.

Once back at the apartments, Trey left for a dentist appointment, and Joanne and Trixie got busy cleaning up the massive mess I had instigated in the kitchen.

It was time for me to come clean as well. I crawled onto the chair, and lifted myself up onto my two hind legs, wincing at the pain. The screen of Joanne's laptop was dark. How did she start it? I'd watched her many times as she typed away, occasionally moving the mouse.

Maybe that was the wakeup alarm. I reached over and gave the mouse a nudge, and then jumped when the screen burst with light and color. What now?

I had never taken a close look at the keyboard, and saw that it was basically the letters of the alphabet arranged in seemingly random order. The words that Joanne typed came a letter at a time. I was amazed, flabbergasted, that she could tap out the words so quickly. She never even looked at the keyboard with its apparently scrambled arrangement of letters. I concluded that I had been grossly underestimating human's abilities.

Using my "thumb" toe, I tentatively tapped at one of the keys. Nothing happened on the screen. I tried another, and again, nothing. Suddenly a window popped up. It was an incoming message from one of Joanne's workmates. On a hunch, I tapped the "enter" key. Now, every time I tapped a key, the associated letter appeared in the window. I suspected that I was composing a response to the message. This would have to do, as long as I was careful not to send off the response.

I wished I knew how that was done so that I could avoid it.

As I laboriously typed out my communication, I thought about my situation—Joanne's new situation. The "special delivery" squad would eventually come looking for me, and would not only terminate me, but possibly Joanne and Trixie as well, depending on the degree of distance between the constitutional ideal and the perceived justification for pragmatic "national security" concerns. It came down to how much Joanne and Trixie knew, or, more correctly, how much the special delivery squad thought they knew. How could I allow Joanne to be harmed for my sake? The only sure approach would be for Joanne and Trixie to know nothing about my unique intelligence. No, that wasn't enough. The special delivery squad wouldn't take any chances. I had to complete the plan concocted by the lab scientists. I would have to somehow return to the lab and allow the autopsy to proceed.

More immediately, I had to erase this message I had been pulling from the nonsensical keyboard letter by hard-won letter.

"Oh—my—God!"

It was Trixie looking over the back of the chair.

"Oh, God!" she yelled, bursting with excitement. "Joanne come here. Now!"

My heart climbed up to thump away in my throat. In my haste to delete the words, I must have bumped the mouse, and moved the activity off the message window, for no matter how I pounded away at the keyboard, nothing changed.

I looked up, and Joanne stood there, staring. Staring. Staring.

I tried to hide what I had written, but my tiny paws were useless to cover the words:

Joanne, I love you.

∞ ∞ ∞ ∞

About the Author

Blaine C. Readler is an electronics engineer, inventor of the FakeTV, and, of course, a writer. He has accumulated a pile of awards, among them, Best Science Fiction in the Beverly Hills Book Awards, two-time Distinguished Favorite in the Independent Press Awards, an IPPY Bronze medal, Honorable Mention in the Eric Hoffer Awards, a finalist for the Foreword Book of the Year, and three-time San Diego Book Awards winner. He lives in San Diego with his wife who has graciously remained married to him for twenty-five years.

He encourages you to visit him:
http://www.readler.com/